A Walk In The Woods

And

Other Short Stories

A WALK IN THE WOODS

AND

OTHER SHORT STORIES

ESTHER CHILTON

I hope you enjoy the stories!

Best wishes,

Esme

A Walk In The Woods

Copyright © Esther Chilton 2018

The right of Esther Chilton to be identified as
author of this work has been
asserted by her in accordance with sections 77 and
78 of the Copyright, Designs
and Patents Act 1988.

All rights reserved. No part of this publication may be reproduced, stored in any retrieval system, copied in any form or by any means, electronic, mechanical, photocopying, recording or otherwise, without written permission from the author. You must not circulate this book in any format.

This is a work of fiction. Names, characters, places and incidents either are products of the author's imagination or are used fictitiously. Any resemblance to actual events, or locales, or persons, living or dead, is entirely coincidental.

ISBN 978 1795725 835

Acknowledgements

An enormous thank you to Charlotte Newton, for designing my beautiful book cover.

I would also like to mention The Writers Bureau. They set me on the path to achieving my dream and for the past ten years, they've given me the opportunity to assist others on their writing journey.

Finally, a big thank you to Graeme for his patience, understanding and support, as well as for helping me in formatting this book and making its publication a reality.

For Charlotte –

Who I will always love, no matter what

Contents

A Walk in the Woods 13

Jake 16

Book Lovers 24

The Letter 30

The Blue Balloon 32

The Brat 33

The Strangest Parents on Earth 37

Dead 45

The Godfather 47

The Battle 51

William 52

Operation Flora 70

A Walk in the Park 77

The Secret Diary of Marvin Martin aged 14 ½ 81

The Lover 83

The Dark Place 90

Home 93

Spaceman Sam 100

If Only 106

Gus 108

About The Author 115

A Walk in the Woods

"Look at that, Jenny. Quick! Over there," I say, my finger jabbing in the air, pointing at the two squirrels darting in and out of the trees.

She laughs, a melodious chuckle bubbling in her throat. Her eyes dance in delight at the spectacle, following the grey blur of fur as the animals race up a tree trunk, disappearing into a sea of brilliant auburns, rusts and coppers. A branch bounces up and down and golden leaves tumble to the ground to nest with others who've found a new home on the forest floor.

I suck in a deep breath. Then blow it out. Tears sting. I push them away. Not now. I won't let them ruin this moment.

The snap of a twig torn in two whips my head round. A man and woman, their arms wrapped around one another, stroll close by before heading down another path.

I turn back to Jenny. I can't see her. Then the rich red of her coat fills my vision. She's stooping to pick up leaves. She chooses a large russet coloured one and twirls the stem round and round in her hand.

"Let's see how many leaves we can carry home. We could make a collage out of them and you could give it to Daddy when he gets home from work. He'd like that."

"What's a collage, Mummy? Is that something to do with school?"

I smile. Such innocence.

"No, darling. It's a picture. We'll make a pretty picture of leaves for Daddy."

"Oooh, yes please!"

Jenny scoops up a handful of leaves and charges off down the path home.

***

I pick up the picture; the paper crunches under my touch and the once glorious garden of riotous autumnal colours merge into one another, as tears trickle down my face, muddying my view. I form a fist with my hand and drag it across my eyes.

But it's no good. A low moan escapes my lips and quickly gains momentum.

Strong arms grip me. For a fleeting second I'm silent, my body rigid at this intrusion.

"Annie, it's okay. It's okay."

David. My body slackens and I allow myself to be absorbed into his hug.

Another man appears – in my mind. John. And Jenny is standing in front of him. His arms are around her waist and he's pulling her to him. They look so happy, so carefree, their mouths pulled back into cheeky grins, their skin glistening with the kiss of the sun. The sea is in the background, a wave rolling in to shore, on pause forever in this photo I have committed to memory.

I've never met John. I don't want to either. I wonder what I'd do if I did. Hit him? Shout at him? Tell him that he shouldn't have been drinking and driving? I know it won't bring Jenny back.

Nor will going to the woods every day. But it'll always be our special place. Mine and Jenny's.

Jake

"Leave my mum alone. Get off her!" Jake shouted. Sweat-soaked clothes stuck to his body, his arms and legs thrashing wildly. Tears fell down his cheeks and he gagged, nausea building. They wouldn't listen. No one would listen.

His eyes opened wide as he stared into the darkness, his nightmare ending. But it wasn't. It was only just beginning. It followed the same pattern every night, mirroring the shocking reality of the week before. That Friday night was one he would never forget.

"What's up with you, Mum? You've not eaten any of your dinner. I know you're a crap cook, but..." Jake had grinned, waiting for his mother to clip him round the ear for his cheek.

"Mum! What's wrong with you? Stop staring at the wall," his voice began to shake. He didn't like the vacant look in her blue-green eyes and her usually soft and shiny hair was hanging in unsightly clumps. And for the first time, he noticed the huge gash across her forehead. "Mum, you're bleeding. And that bruise. Christ!"

The thump at the door made him swing round.

"Who's that now? I bet it's Kev. I told him I wasn't coming out tonight."

"Mrs Bell? Mrs Bell, it's the police. We know you're in there. Please answer the door."

"The police? I've done nothing wrong, Mum.

Honest. Perhaps it's Dad. Maybe…"

"Shut up. Shut up!" his mother yelled.

Jake froze, fear flowing over him at his mother's screeching voice. Her eyes were on stalks, ferocious and frenzied like the cover of the horror book he was reading. Her arms flew up in the air, waving dementedly and vomit spurted out of her mouth.

The flimsy door gave way and policemen dived in, flickering blue lights flashing in the street. Burly arms gripped flesh, hauling Jake's mother to her feet.

"Maureen Bell, I am arresting you on suspicion of murder…"

Murder. His mother had murdered someone. Jake giggled and the room spun. "You reckon my mum has murdered someone? She cries if she hits a rabbit in the road. You've got it wrong, mate."

The policeman continued, "You do not have to say anything…"

Jake's laughter died. They meant it. But they couldn't. *Who* had she murdered?

"Come on, lad. You had best come with us. Is there someone you can stay with?" a fat policeman, his beer belly straining to be free from his uniform, patted him on the shoulder.

That was when he lost it.

***

"There, there, Jake, it's all right. Same nightmare again?"

Jake looked up into his gran's kind face as she ruffled his thick blond hair. "Suppose."

"Jake, come on. You can talk to me. I'm hurting as much as you are. Your mother is my daughter."

Jake stared at her, at the gentle curls framing her heart-shaped face. Mother and daughter were often mistaken for sisters. "But you weren't there, Gran. It was horrible. She went all strange and then they took her away."

"You were a brave boy. You tried to stop them, lad, didn't you?"

"I can't remember. I don't remember anything after Mum went all weird. I just remember waking up here with you the next day."

"I'll look after you, Jake. You're here with me now. Everything will be all right," Gran soothed.

"I want Mum! But she's not coming back, is she? They said she murdered someone. Who did she murder, Gran? Tell me. Please tell me," Jake's voice became a whisper.

Everything in the room was spinning: the old antique chest, the oak bookcase and the picture of the hideous naked woman with rolls of fat.

"It's Dad, isn't it? You said he couldn't be here right now. It's because he's dead. She killed my flippin' dad!"

Darkness descended, blocking out vision and sound. Deeper and deeper he was drowning, his chest expelling air, his arms flailing, his mouth fighting furiously and his mind pleading for salvation.

***

"Thank you for your help, doctor," Gran said, an

hour later.

"That's quite all right. It's an awful lot for a thirteen-year-old boy to cope with. He thinks he's tough, but underneath he's like the rest of us, crying out to be loved. He's going to need a lot of love."

"I know."

"And you, Betty? How are you coping with all this?"

"I don't know, doctor. I really don't. I always hated that husband of hers. A mother always wants the best for her daughter. I told Maureen not to get whickered up with Colin Bell. And then she fell pregnant with Jake. She always said she loved him so what could I do?"

"It's a nasty business."

"It is. I can't believe Colin's dead. It's been a week now. I know I should be sad, but part of me is glad he's gone. But how do I even begin to explain things to the lad? One parent dead and the other accused of his murder," Gran sniffed.

"Don't cry, Betty. I'm sorry, I shouldn't have pried. I just wanted to make sure you were all right."

"I'll be fine, doctor. I've seen all sorts in my life and always got by. I know she's been charged, but I'm sure Maureen will be released soon. There was a queue of people waiting for the right moment to do Colin Bell in. It could have been anyone."

Jake's head was throbbing. They thought he couldn't hear them, but he'd heard every word. His dad was dead. His dad, who was always there to wipe away his tears and dab his wounds whenever he came to harm. His dad with the big blue eyes and mop of unruly brown hair, which made him look like he had just got out of bed. The same dad who was forever there, cheering for him on the football field, be it torrential rain or blistering hot sunshine. His dad, who said Jake would be the one to make them proud. And now he was dead.

His mother's image filled his head. She had killed him, taken away the only dad he had ever known. He knew she had done it. Gran always defended her daughter. But he knew. He had seen it in her eyes.

The tears came, his heart pounding and his whole body hurt, pain and anguish washing over him. Just over a week ago and everything had been all right. He had been looking forward to the funfair, to seeing his mates and having a good laugh.

"It's half-price on Wednesday night, Mum. Kev's going and Matt. Go on, let me go."

"No, Jake. I don't care if it's free rides all night. You've got homework to do. You'll go at the weekend or not at all."

The weekend had come, but by then the fair was the last thing on his mind.

***

"I don't want to go," Jake said a week later.

"Your mum will be heartbroken if you don't go and see her," Gran said, tears in her eyes.

"Oh God, now you're going to start crying again, aren't you? I don't want to go, Gran. She killed my dad. I don't know if I can ever look at her again."

"I know he was your father, Jake. I know you

loved him, but there isn't any proof your mum did it. She'll be home soon. I know it's hard. It's hard for us all."

"You don't know anything," Jake barged past Gran and stomped down the stairs.

He yanked the front door open, enjoying the thunder as it slammed behind him. He stood on the step, his fists clenched, chewed and ragged nails digging into his palms. His legs spurred into action and he was running free, the wind whipping through his hair and rain stabbing his eyes.

His feet took him in the direction of the park and he collapsed onto a swing, his heart hammering as he gripped the stone-cold chain.

"I thought I'd find you here," Gran intruded a short while later, "you always loved the park."

"Leave me alone," Jake looked down at the ground, his feet prodding at an empty Coke can.

"Oh, Jake. Jake."

"You once said you could make everything better. You used to tuck me up at night and kiss my forehead. You said everything would be all right. Well, make this all right."

"I wish I could, Jake."

"Mum's going to prison, isn't she?"

"We don't know that."

"Yes, we do. I'm not stupid, Gran. She did it and they're going to send her away for it. It's not fair. I want my mum."

Gran took him in her arms and stroked his forehead. "I'll look after you, Jake. Whatever happens, I'll look after you. Everything will be okay. You'll see."

***

The building was huge. Jake stared at its ugly façade, bleak and barren. A shiver spread through his body. Barred windows seemed to stare back at him, mocking him, a warning to all who dared enter the gates.

"I told you, Gran. I shouldn't have come. I can't see her. Not in this place."

Gran took his hand and held it tight. "I'm here with you every step of the way."

Both fell silent, each blinking the tears away as they entered the visitors' room. Jake saw the chairs, cheap and coarse like the ones at school. Though, for once, school seemed preferable. Jake fidgeted, his legs swinging to and fro.

"Keep still," Gran said, "look, here she comes."

The hairs on the back of his neck stood to attention. A vice gripped his chest, his breath coming in short, sharp gasps. He had wondered how he would feel when he saw her. His mother, the woman he loved more than anyone else in the world. His mother, his father's killer. Hatred? Fear? Anger? Love?

She walked towards them, a shadow, haunted and haggard. Her eyes came to rest on Jake. A spark ignited in them, burning for a second before the flame was extinguished.

Jake leapt to his feet. "Mum. Mum." He stumbled, clawing his way to her, his arms wide.

"No touching," a prison officer stepped between them.

"She's my mum. Hey, get off me. Mum. Mum!" The tips of his fingers reached out and a tress fell within his grasp. He caressed it before it fell and with it, his mother.

***

"Your mum's okay, Jake," Gran said, as they walked home, "they're looking after her."
"She'll never survive in there, Gran."
"She won't have to."
"You don't really believe that, do you?"
"No, Jake, I don't. But she was driven to it. They'll see that. They've got to."
"You mean Dad made her kill him?"
"I'm sorry, Jake. I didn't mean…I shouldn't have…"
"It's all right, Gran. I know what you mean."
Jake touched his arm, the faded bruise still sore. He thought of his dad. His dad who always wiped away his tears after giving him the beating of his life. His dad who dabbed his wounds, red and raw, while saying over and over again how sorry he was. His dad with the big blue eyes and a mop of unruly brown hair who had always just got out of bed, still drunk from the night before. His dad who cheered him on at football and then gave him a thrashing if he didn't score a goal. The same dad who said Jake would be the one to do well. If he didn't, his dad would throw him out onto the streets.
"I know what Dad was, Gran. I know what he did to Mum. And to me," Jake whispered. "If she hadn't killed him first, I would have, one day."

He allowed himself to be wrapped in Gran's arms, safe and warm.

"We'll wait for her, won't we, Gran? Whatever happens, we'll be here when she comes home."

Book Lovers

Stop it! No, no, no. Not now, not while she's watching. Daniel forced his hands into his lap.

He had almost done it – almost revealed his fetish in front of her. He looked at his chewed nails and tugged at a strand of loose skin. All around him, in the crowded and chatty student café, life carried on, oblivious to the churnings of Daniel Bradman's mind.

He lifted one bottom cheek, feeling the numbness setting in after perching on the stiff seat for half an hour. His hand moved, creeping up the table to the very top. It took on a life of its own and grabbed the brand-new textbook. *No!* For a moment, he thought he had spoken aloud and his eyes scanned the sea of faces. They stopped. He found her, two tables in front. She was looking right at him. He turned away. Thank goodness he hadn't succumbed to his greed.

He dared to look back at her. Her eyes hadn't left his and she was smiling. Kathy Roberts was smiling - at him. He could feel the Ferrari-red flush on his cheeks and he looked down to find his hands in his lap once more.

Kathy Roberts. She was a first-year student studying sociology. He had spent hours deliberating over the choice of sociology or psychology. He knew he should have gone for sociology. He gnawed at the inside of his lip. It was a daft reason to opt for a degree course, one that could affect his whole life, but it was Kathy Roberts.

He felt as if he had been in love with Kathy Roberts forever, instead of the month he had known her. If you could call furtive glances at someone 'knowing' them.

A chair scraped back and heels clacked, coming closer. Footsteps stopped beside his table. Daniel's head wouldn't come up. It was Kathy. He would know her boots anywhere. They were beautiful brown leather with laces to match, but giant fluffy teddy slippers would have had the same effect.

He could hardly breathe. He was going to do it - he was going to look at her. Slowly at first, then with great guts, he thrust his head up. Too late! As he stared at her retreating back, he thought what a lovely butterfly clip she had in her long dark hair.

Daniel punched out his breath. What was wrong with him? He knew he stood no chance with her, especially when she found out the truth, but surely he could cope with looking at her? It didn't help being so shy, but it was the book thing that was really letting him down.

His eyes sidled back to the textbook. She had gone now, so what did it matter? Would anyone notice a mousy haired youth and a book? His nostrils flared. He could smell the sumptuous scent.

"All right, Daniel? You've already got that book, then? You're keen," Ashley Nugent said, pulling out a chair and making himself comfortable.

Daniel was choking, gulping in great pockets of air. Ashley reluctantly dragged himself from the chair and whacked Daniel on the back. Daniel thanked him by way of a thumbs-up.

"Must be something in the air," Ashley said, sitting back down.

Go away. Just go away. Daniel glared at his fellow student, who was now ordering a glass of tap water from the pink-haired waitress. *I want to be on my own. I need to do it. I can't stand it any longer.*

"Perhaps I could borrow that book for a bit? I must get myself some money. I could get a Saturday job, I suppose," Ashley said, slumping lower in the seat and taking a slurp from the chipped glass.

Daniel tried to focus as the room spun. Borrow the book? Take it away from him, when he, Daniel, hadn't even christened it?

"I've seen some job adverts in the window. You could have a look at them. NOW!"

Daniel said, clasping his book to his chest, then calming down, "This book isn't that expensive. You'll save up for it in no time."

Ashley looked at him, a frown on his face, but he made no effort to move. Seconds. Then minutes went by. Daniel didn't think Ashley was ever going to move. He had to, otherwise he was going to witness the act, that very act he had battled to remain hidden throughout his school years.

Daniel sighed. This wasn't how it was supposed to be. University was a fresh start, miles away from anyone who knew him. He had thought he could master it. He should have known.

"I'll see you later, mate," Ashley said, moving off in the direction of the window.

Daniel's heart was doing dive-bombs into a tiny paddling pool. His eyes darted from table to table.

Students were leaving, heading to various lectures. Daniel knew he should be going too.

The book was on fire, igniting in his arms. Slowly, he lowered it to the table. It was calling to him, begging him to do it. It wouldn't wait any longer. He closed his eyes, his whole body trembling as the need took over.

He held the book out and his eyes flew open. A smile played at the corner of his lips, spreading into a huge grin. He opened the first page and brought the book up to his face. He closed his mouth and took a deep breath in through his nose. The crisp, fresh aroma tickled his nostrils, before attacking him and shooting straight up. Succulent. Sharp. Sweet. His jaw dropped in ecstasy and he let the breath glide out. It definitely scored an eight out of ten.

He leaned back in his chair. The best part was yet to come. His tongue flicked over his teeth, pushing through the tiny gap until it writhed like a snake, toying and teasing its prey. He held the book closer and his tongue lengthened, barely an inch from the page.

Daniel's eyes danced, taking in the fine finish of the paper and the bold words blurring into one. He closed his eyes and ran his tongue from the bottom to the top of the page in one almighty lick. His taste buds were on fire, savouring its tangy taste. Another eight out of ten. Not bad but a bit of a disappointment if he was honest. He had thought this one would be a nine. Maybe one day he would find that ten.

Daniel still had his eyes closed when he realised

he was not alone. The soft, "Ahem," had turned into a, "What on earth do you think you're doing?"

He opened one eye. Kathy. He closed it again. Maybe she wasn't really there. He opened both eyes. She was and she looked as if she had gone into shock. Daniel didn't need to ask how much she had seen, though he had to admit even witnessing a small part was enough to cause anyone concern.

He thought about lying. There were chocolate crumbs inside the book and he was a chocoholic or perhaps he could say it was part of a psychology experiment he had been set.

Daniel's churning stomach had now churned down to the deepest depths. He had to face facts. He had blown it. The truth was out.

"I was coming over to ask you out. I realise what a huge mistake I've made. I mean, I stopped at your table earlier and you wouldn't even look at me. It's obvious you don't like me," Kathy's voice was starting to crack. "If you're doing that thing with the book to put me off you…"

"No. No!" Daniel was on his feet. "I do like you. A lot. It's just…I'm shy."

She liked him! Kathy Roberts liked him and wanted to go out with him. But the book. He had to explain about the book. He tried to think logically. Everything was going to be all right. The psychology experiment sounded plausible, didn't it?

Daniel looked into Kathy's face. Seconds passed, turning into minutes.

"Before I ask you out again, what were you doing with that book?"

She asked. She had to ask. Chocolate or

psychology?

"If you go out with me, you'll find out sooner or later anyway. Well...I have this thing...about books. I like to sniff them and lick them," Daniel said, knowing that to his own ears he sounded like a madman.

Kathy smiled. "Is that all? For a moment I thought you had some weird fetish. I think there's something you need to know about me. I eat books. Not the whole book but just the corner of each page. I like first edition paperbacks best. They're so tender. I can't resist them."

Daniel frowned. She ate books? She actually destroyed the pristine and perfect page? He wasn't sure how he felt about that. A shiver shot through him. Life was full of hard decisions, though this one was going to be easier than many he had made. After all, it *was* Kathy Roberts.

The Letter

My darling Clarissa,

I feel sick as I write this letter – a letter you'll never see. But I have to write it – I *need* to write it.

I watched you yesterday – watched you pick up the threadbare teddy, lovingly caressing its coarse chest. "I must go and find Sarah. We're going to have a tea party," you cried, eagerly scrambling to your feet.

Then you saw me. Your brow wrinkled and your shoulders started to shake. "Who are you?" you demanded, your hands folding into fists.

I stared back at you, the tears already falling.

"I don't know you. You shouldn't be here. Daddy! Help!" with each word, your voice grew.

The punch caught me on the arm. I stood there, in the doorway to our bedroom, our bedroom of fifty-one years, and did nothing. I knew I'd bruise. I always did.

I grabbed you. Tight. For an instant, you knew me and your face softened. Your eyes danced with that look. Love.

Then it was gone and the hardness and hatred were back. I felt the warmth of your spittle as it oozed down my face. My arms unlocked from yours and you pushed past me, a girlish giggle escaping from your lips.

I wonder if I can go through it again. Day after

day. Only each day it worsens. But I will. For you, my love, for you.

For better, for worse,

Yours Frederick

The Blue Balloon

Sally hated the blue balloon. She stared at it, tears falling freely down her face. She stabbed it with her nail, wanting to burst it, to banish it from her mind. But up it bounced, drifting gently towards her.

She pushed it away, then pulled at her sweater sleeves before wrapping her arms round herself. Thoughts and images whirled through her mind. *What if...*

"Sally…" a voice softly spoke. Hands reached out.

She turned away from her husband.

"Sally!" more urgent this time.

She clenched her fists, swinging round.

"If you hadn't insisted on going off and buying that balloon, he wouldn't have tried to follow you…" her breath caught in her throat.

This time, she allowed the arms to enfold her and the loving lips to brush her hair.

"It'll be okay. I promise."

But how could he promise? *How?*

"Mummy! Blue balloon!"

Her head snapped up, her eyes searching the scene before her and finding khaki trousers and a red top.

"Blue balloon!" the little boy said, his eyes bright, pushing past his mother and making a grab for the balloon.

The Brat

Alarm bells ring. I groggily reach out, thumping the offending object. Peace. At last.

"Jacob! You'll be late for school," Mum's shrill voice tears through my sleep.

I dare to open one eye. Sunlight stabs me. I open the other eye, my head hurting.

"Jacob!" Mum is beside me now.

"I'm up. I'm up. It's not my fault the brat kept me awake last night."

"She's not a brat. She's your baby sister. And her name's Megan."

Mum pulls the covers back. I grimace, stumbling out of bed. I hate Monday mornings.

Having satisfied Mum that I've washed and cleaned my teeth, I make my way downstairs. I cringe, catching sight of the brat. She's sitting in her high chair, cereal plastered round her mouth. She becomes excited, staring up at me and she begins to beat out a tune with her plastic spoon.

"See, she loves you," Mum encourages me.

"Well, I hate her."

I give the brat my best glare. She smiles at me, babbling in her stupid language.

"She can't even talk. All she does is dribble and scream and she stinks."

"She's a baby, Jacob. And you were like that once."

"Yeah, right."

Mum sighs.

"Anyway," I continue, "you didn't answer my question. Why did you want another kid? If it was to stop Dad leaving, then it didn't work very well, did it? It just made him go off with that tart, that's what it did."

I chew my lip, hardly daring to look as Mum bursts into tears. I grab my school bag, my eyes falling on the boiled egg on the kitchen table. "And I've told you before. I don't have egg and soldiers anymore. I'm fifteen, not five." I walk to the door, yanking it open and the glass shudders as I slam it shut.

The day drags as all days spent looking at the whiteboard do. I punch the air. It's half-past three. Time to go home at last. But home to what?

I dawdle along the pavement, kicking at a half empty can. The brown-black liquid squelches out onto the ground to merge with other vile, unknown substances.

I turn the corner, pausing to stare at my house. For a moment, there's the threat of tears. I sniff. I won't cry. I walk on. I have nowhere else to go.

Loud wails fill the air. A car skids. An ambulance is in sight. It stops. The paramedics rush in.

"Mum," the cry catches in my throat. Now I am running, staggering to reach her.

The front door is open. "Mum!" She is screaming. I am by her side, watching as she thrashes her arms and shrieks hysterically. My eyes are drawn to the lifeless form. The brat is pale and yet so peaceful. She lies still, unaware of the panic she is causing.

I hug Mum. She pushes me away and follows the two men out the door. I run upstairs, collapsing on the bed as her last words ring in my ears, "It's your fault, Jacob! It's all your fault!"

Hours pass. I can't wait any longer. I go to the hospital. Mum and I stare at the baby. A lump forms in my throat as tubes and wires all colours of the rainbow poke out from the tiny body. I look up to the huge machines, bleeping in confirmation that Megan is still alive.

I pace up and down the room, searching for words of comfort, searching for words I don't believe.

"We're doing our best," the doctors said. We all know what that means. Mum touches my shoulder.

"I'm sorry, love. I didn't mean what I said. It's just…it's just so hard," she says, her voice breaking, "with your father leaving…"

I turn to her, looking at the familiar brown hair curling over her forehead, the deep dark eyes usually full of life and the beautiful face now tear-streaked and bloated. My own tears merge with hers, her strong arms around me. I hug her close, feeling the warmth and love of my mother.

Holding hands, we walk over to Megan. I squeeze Mum's fingers, closing my eyes. I imagine the little figure coming to life, a giggle emerging and her eyes opening to stare at me, full of love for her older brother.

The machines are going mad. My eyes are wide open. Doctors, nurses, the room is full. We are ushered away.

We wait for an eternity. I catch Mum's eye and look away. We both know what's happened.

The doctor is suddenly in front of us. His face reveals nothing. He breaks into a smile. My heart beats wildly. I listen to his words and battle to stop myself hugging him.

I look down at my little sister, so frail, so perfect, so in need of my love. She was never the brat; I was the brat.

I glance at Mum. She grins at me. I'm sure the brat will rear his ugly head again. We teenagers are always told we're nothing but trouble. Though for the time being, we're a family once more: Mum, me and Megan against the world.

The Strangest Parents on Earth

Harry always knew his parents were strange. But when he saw them change colour and shape, he knew they were *really* strange.

Up until that moment, that very moment when he had opened the door to their bedroom, he had thought they were like everyone else's parents. Everyone's parents were strange. Parents belonged to another world. A world of completely and utterly no dress sense or hair sense. They liked watching old films. Films no one other than adults had ever heard of and listening to music from a bygone age, where all the singers wore dreadful clothes and hats.

Adults also thought they could dance. Shuffling from side to side and waving their arms around like a demented puppet was not dancing. Yet they all thought they were still so cool and clever. But as soon as they were shown some homework questions, they went all funny and started mumbling and making excuses.

They couldn't talk properly either – only nonsense to each other. When they started to talk to anyone under the age of sixteen, their voices went all squeaky and they began talking about fluffy bunnies.

The worst thing was when they said, "We were young once." Perhaps they had been, but growing into an adult obviously wiped out all memory of it.

Harry's parents were exactly like that.

"When we were your age, we spent exciting weekends round the camp fire singing songs and eating proper food. McDonald's was a farm in our day with sheep and cows, not those dreadful nugget things. We knew how to have real fun. We weren't worried about complicated computers and mobile phones."

Now he knew why.

He hadn't known what to do at first. Not seeing a sight such as that. He knew he didn't want his parents to know he was there. They always told him to knock first. He didn't mind that; they knocked before they came into his room after all. Though he hadn't knocked today – because they weren't supposed to be there.

They were supposed to be at work. Mum behind the counter at the post office and Dad putting his hand down the loo to rid someone of an unspeakable blockage.

Harry knew he should be at school, but that was beside the point. He had only nipped out to get his homework. He'd spent ages doing it and had just forgotten to put it into his school bag. Old Slater would go mad if he didn't hand it in.

He had almost made it too. The exercise book was still in his hands. He had reached the stairs and was ready to go down when he heard the noise. It was faint at first, more like a whistle and then it grew louder and more gobbly, if there was such a word, but that's the only way Harry could describe it. Yes, like a load of turkeys making manic gobble noises.

He had to look. Anyone would have done the

same. He wasn't frightened when he tiptoed up to the door. Well, he was, though he wasn't about to admit he was afraid of something which sounded like a turkey.

Harry pushed the door, gently at first. He poked his head round and he was certain his jaw had slammed down to the floor and flown back up into his face.

He knew it was his mum and dad instantly. Dad still looked like his dad – big and bald with a goatee beard that was trying its best to look trendy and failing abysmally. The only problem was that his dad was now a big, bald, bearded pig.

If that wasn't enough to take in, his mum, who still had big, brown eyes and slim legs, was a deer. A very beautiful deer but a deer nonetheless.

The gobbling was building and threatening to burst Harry's eardrums. Suddenly, they stopped. Silence. Then they did it. It was the weirdest thing Harry had ever seen. He was surprised he didn't faint.

First his dad changed from pale pink to peach and then purple. Orange spots exploded onto his body. His legs slowly shrank to leave a blob of a body and finally his head exploded and contracted like a balloon sucked dry of air. Hundreds of eyes popped onto the tiny head.

Harry tore his eyes away from his dad to his mum. The soft, brown coat merged to grey, brightening and finally staying a rich red. Green diamonds dashed onto her skin. Her legs began to disappear, though something stayed, still slender, which Harry was sure could be called legs at a push.

The eyes were still brown, though her two had now been joined by many others.

It was then that Harry realised his parents were literally from out of this world. But they weren't really his parents. His parents weren't aliens.

"Yes, we are," his dad's voice boomed into Harry's head, "you were born on the planet Zuma, just like us, though you were only a little baby when we came to earth so I doubt you remember."

Harry jumped and fell back, landing on his bottom. The exercise book flew from his hands. It didn't seem so important now.

"Not so loud," Mum's voice now, pushing its way into his mind. "Sorry, dear. Your father has always been too loud. Now, I think you had better come in."

"No. What have you done to my parents?" Harry asked.

"Well done, dear. We didn't even have to teach you. This is going to be so much easier than I thought," Mum again, still in his head.

"What's going to be easier?" Harry stopped. He was talking to his parents without saying a word. He was also aware that he was talking in the gobble language, though it suddenly made perfect sense to him.

But it couldn't be. None of it could be happening. His parents were normal, boring people who used to go camping.

"We didn't really, dear. We read that somewhere in an earth book."

He felt sick. Very, very sick.

"Just wait until you learn how to change minds

as well, Harry. It's terrific," Dad butted in.

"One step at a time, dear. Now, Harry, are you coming in or do we have to fetch you?"

Harry gulped. He got up and willed his feet to move in the opposite direction. They weren't having any of it. His mum and dad were coming for him. He knew it.

But they weren't. They weren't moving at all. But he was – right towards them. He reached out to grab at the door before sliding gracefully through it and landing at their feet.

"You really ought to be getting back to school with your homework, Harry. Though I suppose you're in no fit state to now, are you?" Mum asked.

Harry was about to ask her how she knew when he realised that she knew everything. He squirmed and shuffled his feet from one spot to another. He didn't particularly like the idea of his parents knowing everything he was thinking. Perhaps there was a way to block it.

"Harry!" Mum said aloud. "Stop that."

"The boy's gifted," Dad laughed and hands shot out from the top of his head and joined together in a loud clap.

Harry backed away. He wasn't like them. He wasn't.

"You're a mouse in your earth form," Mum said, proudly.

That was typical. A weedy little mouse. He knew he had a small nose and he was always twitching it, sniffing the snot back up. He had small hands and feet too and long fingers and toes like claws. He stopped himself. He didn't. He didn't.

"This is my earth form. I'm a boy," he shouted. "Not that I've got an earth form."

"Yes, you have. I knew we should have told you about all this sooner, but the Council thought it wise to wait until you were a little bit older. You see, the Great Council of Zuma sent us on a mission to study earth for a hundred earth years. That's not long in Zuma years. Anyway, they said we needed to disguise ourselves."

"As animals?" Harry asked.

"They get everything wrong. We didn't realise at first. Your dad spent three weeks covered in muck in a pigsty. Human forms are much better but so primitive."

"Well, I like my form just as it is, thank you very much. I don't think much of your blubbery mass of blancmange," Harry said, defiantly.

"I think it's time we showed him what he really looks like, don't you?" Mum said, smiling at Dad.

Not that Harry was actually sure she was smiling, but he thought the long, curved line stuck in the middle of her face looked like a mouth and a smile.

Suddenly, Harry didn't care if she was smiling. His body was shrinking. His rib cage felt as if it was being crushed and he was sure someone was jumping up and down on his head. Then he began shaking uncontrollably as if a hundred people were continually poking him.

He looked down. He didn't have any legs and his body was green with yellow stripes swirling madly across it. His hands. Where were his hands? Oh yes, at the side of his head.

Harry gazed around the room, amazed that he didn't have to turn his head to see everything in it. It was all so clear and then he remembered his eyes had multiplied by a few hundred.

"Look at him," Mum said, proudly and reached out her hands to stroke him. "I've wished for this day for so long."

It was almost as bad as when she ruffled his hair. Not that he seemed to have hair anymore.

"I can tell he's going to be a natural at flying. I've always wanted to teach my son how to fly," Dad said, joining in with the stroking.

Flying? He was going to learn how to fly? Suddenly, he didn't mind them stroking him one little bit.

"And I rather think he'll like learning to drive," Mum said.

What was she talking about? He had years to go until he could learn to drive.

"Driving for us is a little bit different to driving for humans. We also prefer to travel by speedsound rather than by car," she continued.

"Speedsound?"

"The vehicles are so fast humans can't see them," Dad said, excitedly.

Harry grinned. He liked the sound of that very much. He had to admit that the day hadn't got off to a very good start and it did feel a bit weird to find out that he was an alien, but perhaps it wouldn't be so bad. It would be great for scaring the girls and he could change old Slater's mind about the homework situation.

"No, we do not use our special gifts for that sort

of thing," Mum spoke into his head.

Harry blocked her out and she folded her arms in front of her mouth, tutting. He smiled. He could nip across to Disneyland in no time at all whenever he liked. He had always wanted to go to the moon too, but a new planet was even better.

To top it all, his mum and dad weren't half as bad as he had thought they were. In fact, he could safely say that he had the coolest family on earth.

Dead

I didn't think looking down upon oneself when dead would be quite like this. In fact, I didn't believe in all that. Once you're dead, you're dead; aren't you?

I look at my face, so pale and my eyes, insignificant and lost amongst the dense drama of lashes. The slash across my mouth; Blood Red, the lipstick's called. God, what a state. How did I let it come to this?

Then I see him. He's standing on the spot, right by the bed, his hands clasped together, the knuckles bone white. His head tips back and a growl escapes, gaining momentum with each grunt. His fingers escape their prison and grab at his hair. In moments he's spent and slips to the floor.

Drip, drip, drip. The sound demands my attention. I find the source. I liked that top. Mum was with me when I tried it on.

"Green's your colour. Go on, I'll treat you," she'd said, giving my arm a squeeze.

That stain will never come out. I watch the trail of blood, snaking its way from the cotton, over the sheets, spattering the wooden floor.

"Where did you get that bruise from?" I can still hear the catch in Mum's voice. "He'll really hurt you one day." I ignored the tears. Told her she didn't know what she was talking about.

A flash of silver on the bed. Smoked Scottish salmon fillets, tender belly pork – the knife has seen it all. And to think I moaned that it was getting a little blunt.

A flicker of movement. A finger. Mine. Now two. My hands wrap round the knife. I can't see myself anymore, but I don't need to. I'm not done yet. But you are, you bastard. I'm coming for you.

The Godfather

His head hurt like mad. He lay there a while on the cold concrete, his eyes closed. How long had he been there? A day? Two? What had happened? Who was he? He didn't even know his own name. He gulped back the tears.

Then froze. He wasn't alone. Someone had hurt him and now they had come back. They were getting closer. He braced himself for a fist to come flying or...a tongue to lick his face?

He forced his eyes open, fighting against the persistent pain. It was a cat. He smiled, despite himself. He liked cats, even mangy old cats like this one. There, that was something else he knew about himself. Any minute now, his name, address, date of birth and school would explode into his head.

He waited. Nothing.

"Who am I?" he shouted.

The cat stopped its ferocious licking and hopped off him huffily. Did cats get huffy and if they did, why was this one huffy?

The cat had to be a she. She was even worse than his mum. A grin spread. He was beginning to remember! He couldn't picture his mum though, but he knew she nagged him. A lot.

He looked around. He was in an alleyway - a shortcut to somewhere. Maybe a shortcut home.

His eyes came to rest on the cat, now with its nose stuck up in the air too.

"Blimey, you are worse than my mum. I was only asking who I am. I wasn't shouting at you," he said.

The cat turned round and shrugged its shoulders. The boy's mouth gaped open. Cats didn't shrug their shoulders and cats didn't understand human words either.

He shook his head, trying to clear the fog. The cat started meowing.

"Stop that. You're making my head throb," he said.

The meowing stopped.

"Ok, so you can understand more than most cats. Bet you can't tell me my name, can you?"

The cat started to nod its head.

"Great, my name's Noddy," the boy said, touching his head. He took his hand away, disappointed not to find a very large lump there. Something had to explain what he was doing in an alleyway, battered and bruised and talking to a cat.

Then it came to him.

"You're not nodding. You're bobbing your head up and down. My name's Bob," he said.

The cat meowed and launched itself on him, rewarding him with a loud purr. Bob's shoulders slumped. He looked down at his clothes. His trainers were trendy, his jeans were baggy and his top was the 'in' colour, he was certain of it. Bobs wore frumpy trousers, stiff shirts, silly shoes and khaki cardigans. Bobs were at least sixty years old and he was fifteen. What on earth had his mum and dad been playing at calling him Bob?

His hands flew to his jeans' pocket. A wallet

would be in there - an address, a phone – a way to get home. Nothing.

"I'm never going to get home," he said.

A flurry of fur caught his eye.

"Don't leave me," Bob said.

The cat was almost round the corner now. Then it stopped, turned to him and waved its paw to beckon him forward.

"I'm coming. What are you, my Fairy Godmother?" Bob asked.

A hiss came from between barred teeth.

"Sorry, Fairy Godfather?"

The hiss fizzled out and the teeth were gone from view. Instead, a gigantic grin had taken their place.

"As long as it gets me home, I suppose I can sort out the 'seeing a Fairy Godfather cat thing' later. What are my mum and dad like?" Bob asked when his saviour stopped to scratch its ear.

The nose wrinkled and the ears flattened.

"A bit weird?"

The head went on one side.

"A lot weird. But are they kind? Am I happy at home?"

The head nodded vigorously before the cat swivelled round and darted off again. Bob followed.

So, he was happy at home, but would he ever get home? Of course he wouldn't. Not if he was talking to a cat who thought it understood humans. It probably hadn't been fed for days and when it had seen Bob, it thought Christmas had come early. No wonder it was trying to get him moving. It wanted some food, shelter and a warm place to stay.

But they already had three dogs, five cats, a

budgie, two rabbits, two guinea pigs, seven goldfish and a tortoise. Bob laughed. Another thing remembered.

He stared at the sullen face.

"You knew what I was thinking, didn't you? I'm sorry, I didn't mean it, but I just want to go home," he said.

This time the tears fell. More images came - of a hand on his shoulder and a smiley face - Mum - of a pat on the back and a proud look in the eye - Dad.

Still more flashes came. Not so pleasant this time – of boys standing round him.

Poking him, pulling him, punching him and taking his wallet and phone. Next came the pain, blinding him until he blacked out.

Sobs swept through his whole body and he stopped, his shoulders shaking. He jumped at the sound of a door opening. Cries and screams filled the air. Bob looked at his saviour. He smiled, sure the cat winked and certain a sparkle of shimmering dust had shot up into the sky.

Then arms grabbed him. Hands ruffled his hair. Lips kissed him. He allowed himself to become lost in their love. Tears came once more, but this time for a very different reason. He let the strong arms lead him inside. He glanced back, searching for the cat, but the cat was nowhere to be seen.

The Battle

Billy loved life – clambering up trees and clinging to trunks, a pirate on lookout duty, ready to report any scallywags trying to board ship; or hurtling along on his bike, legs peddling furiously, tongue out, a famous motorbike racer, vying for the lead.

"Try not to worry," he said to his parents, as he tugged the duvet right up to his chin, his eyelids drooping. "I'll be all right. I've always wanted to float on a fluffy cloud. It'll be so much fun and you and Dad will be able to look up and up into the sky and know that I'll be there, waving down at you."

Rachel, his mother, listened at the foot of the stairs. Silence. No tinkling chuckle as he told a joke to a friend, no triumphant roar as crusades were fought on the X-Box. She gulped. She wasn't going to cry; she wasn't. Her shoulders shook, the wails escaping her body, arguing otherwise.

Yesterday, Billy lost his battle with cancer.

William

Mummy has gone mad. I don't like her like this. She's pulling at her hair and stamping her feet. Now she's crying. I'm crying too.

"Mummy?" I take a step towards her.

"George? George, is that you?" her blue eyes stare into mine.

"No, Mummy, it's Anne. Daddy's not here."

"No!" her screams are as loud as the air-raid siren. "Bring him back. Do you hear me? George!" She shakes me.

I hope I am dreaming a horrible, horrible dream. I try to open my eyes, but they are already open. My nightmare is real.

"Joan, what's going on?" Mrs Edwards from two doors down bangs on the window.

"No. Please, no," Mummy lets me go and falls to the ground.

"Joan. Oh my goodness," Mrs Edwards is in the room, "Anne, you're as white as a sheet. What's happened?"

"Mummy…" I am trembling and I can't see out the mist of tears hanging over me.

"I'd better fetch the doctor. You stay there, Anne," Mrs Edwards says.

"It was this letter. She read this and then she went all funny," I pick up the piece of paper from the floor and hand it to her.

"Missing, presumed killed," she mumbles.

"Anne, I'm so sorry."

***

Minutes. Hours. Days pass. I don't know. And I don't care. All I know is that my daddy is dead and my mummy has been taken away. A 'breakdown' they said. They won't let me see her. I want my mummy and I want my daddy.

I open my eyes. Darkness is all around me. Strange shapes move around the room and a tiny light dances on the ceiling. I reach out for teddy. He always makes me feel better. He's not there. I start screaming and I can't stop.

"There, there, Anne. You've had a bad nightmare, that's all. You're safe now," the voice is soft. Arms hug me close.

"Mummy?"

"It's me, love. Mrs Edwards. You're going to stay with Peter and me for a bit. Just until your mummy gets better."

Peter's my best friend. He's older than me. He's nine. He can be quite bossy at times, but he's all right.

"My daddy's dead, isn't he?"

"We don't know that, love. Don't give up hope. There's always hope."

"Is Mr Edwards dead?"

"No! Well, I don't think so. He's fine. Yes, he's fine," Mrs Edwards sounds stern.

"Will Mummy die?"

"No, Anne, the special doctors are taking care of her. She'll be home soon, you'll see."

I close my eyes and this time I am dreaming. It's a dream of me, Mummy and Daddy. We are eating a picnic with lots and lots of cake and biscuits. Daddy takes me in his arms. My daddy is so handsome with huge, brown eyes like teddy. He swings me round and round. I laugh, grinning at Mummy. She pokes at a blonde curl flying free from her head and weaves it over her ear. We are so happy, so very happy.

***

"Anne!" fingers prod me and a face is almost touching mine. It is a big, round face with ginger hair. Peter.

"Peter Edwards, leave Anne alone," Mrs Edwards joins us.

"What's she doing here, Mum?" What's wrong with her house?"

"Peter!"

"My daddy's dead and my mummy has gone mad."

"Oh," Peter backs away, his face bright red.

I begin to cry again and Peter runs from the room.

"I'm sorry, love. It'll be all right," Mrs Edwards stands in the doorway.

Daddy says Mrs Edwards knows everything about everyone. Like the time when the man from over the road was having 'a fair' with the lady from number two. Whatever that means. She also knew when Daddy fell over and sprained his ankle. Daddy says she peers in the window all the time.

But I like Mrs Edwards. She smells of apple pie and cream.

"Come on, love, let's get you dressed. Then we'll have a bit of breakfast. You've got to keep your strength up for your mum. She'll be home soon," Mrs Edwards pulls me away from the window.

"Can I see her? Will you take me to see Mummy?"

"Not today, Anne. But I promise you we'll see her soon."

***

"Hurry up, Anne. For gawd's sake! Let's go over the field. Come on, I'll chase you," Peter shouts as I join him outside.

We push the gate, running through it and we are free, free from the horrible war. I stop and stare at a squirrel scurrying for the cover of trees. My eyes sting with tears. Daddy and me always went out for walks across the fields looking for squirrels and rabbits. Daddy said I could have a rabbit of my own one day.

"What's up with you?" Peter runs up to me.

"Nothing," I run past, blinking the tears away. Nothing will ever be the same again. I run like I have never run before. Sweat is pouring down my face, but I don't care. I shall run forever.

I can hear voices. Laughter. I stop, but my legs are still moving. I fall, my hands reaching out to save myself. I feel pain. Fear. Someone is coming.

"Hey, little girl, are you okay?"

I am trembling, unable to look up and see the owner of the strange voice. Arms reach out. He touches me and I feel sick.

"Come on, little one, let's get you up on your feet."

My face shoots up and I meet his. It's a man like Daddy. He's dressed smartly in uniform, but he doesn't talk like Daddy and now I think about it, his uniform is a lot smarter than Daddy's.

"Wow," Peter has caught up. "Who are you? Are you real?"

The soldier laughs and his face is all smiles. "Of course I am, son. I'm from America."

"A real G.I.? Mum said there was an American army camp near here. Can we see it? Can we?" Peter grins.

"Another time. I've got to head back. Hey, want some gum?"

Peter grabs the stick offered. I stare up into the stranger's face. He's not as handsome as my daddy, but he's tall and his hair is brown too.

"You want some, little girl? Hey, you don't look so good. Are you okay?" he bends down towards me.

His face changes and Daddy's here. I smile. My daddy has come home.

"Anne," Peter pokes me.

Daddy has gone again. The American is in his place.

"Anne? That's a pretty name. I'm William."

"And I'm Peter. Do you live in Hollywood? Mum says all the movie stars live there," Peter says, his jaw chomping on the gum.

William winks at me. "Sure, son, I live in Hollywood. I know most of the film stars. Clark Gable, why he lives next door. Anyway, nice meeting you. Maybe I'll see you around."
As quickly as he appeared, William has gone.
"Wow, wasn't he terrific? A real American. Come on, let's go home. I want to tell Mum."
Peter runs on and he too, disappears from view. I follow, a slow walk, my legs heavy and tired. It seems to take forever to get back.
"Anne! Anne! One of their jeeps went right by the house. What kept you?" Peter holds the gate open for me and I see that Mrs Edwards is in the garden too. "Isn't it great, Mum?"
"Well, we don't know much about these Americans," she says.
"But he had gum," Peter insists.
"We'll see. Anne, are you all right, love?"
"I'm fine thank you, Mrs Edwards. Do you think William knows what happened to my daddy?"
"Oh, Anne. Let's go and have some lunch." Mrs Edwards hugs me. It feels nice.

***

That afternoon and the next and the one after that, we are drawn to the American camp. I see William, but he doesn't know anything about Daddy.
I didn't like William at first, but he gave me some soap and he gets me ice cream, so he's not so bad. William is taking us to see some planes now.
"This one is a Flying Fortress," William says proudly. "It can drop a bomb into a pickle barrel

from twenty thousand feet."

"That's the best ever. What about that one?" Peter points at a huge, ugly plane.

"A troop carrier, Peter," William says and they walk towards it.

Their voices fade and I stand alone, watching and waiting for Peter to return. I stare at the Flying Fortress. I see its mighty engines roaring and it is up in the air. The pilot is dashing and everyone loves him. He turns to look at me. I see him. It's Daddy. He is waving.

Laughter interrupts me. I swing round. It's Peter. I look back to the Flying Fortress, its wheels firmly on the ground.

Peter clicks his fingers and hums a tune. "Bet you don't know what it is. It's Fats Waller. William taught me. Isn't it cool?"

I don't reply and we walk home. Mrs Edwards greets us, a nervous look on her face.

"There's someone here to see you, Anne," she says, taking my hand.

Suddenly I feel very cold. Something tells me to run away, but I can't.

"It's your mother, love. She's better now," Mrs Edwards strokes my hand.

"She's back? And she's better? But I thought you said she was going to stay with the special people for a while."

"Well, it has been two months, Anne."

A lump forms in my throat. The time has sped by. I walk into the house and break into a smile. Mummy is home. Mummy will make everything better.

"Mummy!" I burst into the room, my arms outstretched.

Mummy is sitting there on a chair. She looks at me. Her blue eyes are dull and drab. She is white, so white I can almost see through her.

"Mummy?"

"Anne, darling," she gets up and hugs me close. "I'm sorry, Anne. I'm so sorry."

"Mummy, are you better now?"

Silence.

Mummy finds her voice. "Yes, Anne, much better."

My hands can feel her bones. Her skin is so thin and her bones are poking out.

Mummy is lying.

"What did they do?" I ask.

"Who?"

"The doctors, Mummy. Did they give you some medicine?"

"Yes, plenty of medicine…"

"What else?"

"Anne, why do you ask?" she is getting angry.

I pull away. She's going to have a fit again.

"Mummy, I'm sorry. I didn't mean anything."

"It's all right, Anne. They just did a few other things, things to make me feel better," Mummy has calmed down. "Come on, let's get your bits together and go home."

Ten minutes later, we are home. I gaze at the walls I know so well and yet I feel like I haven't seen them before. I walk to the sideboard and search for Daddy's photo. I stroke his face, the face I will never see again.

Mummy places her hands on my shoulder. "Anne, oh, Anne."

I bury my head in her blouse, listening to her heartbeat. I let myself cry. I can't do anything else. Mummy cries too and we stand there for a very long time.

***

Eight months have passed since my daddy died. Sometimes, when I go across the fields to see William, I talk to Daddy. I tell him that Mummy is starting to laugh again and her bones don't poke through quite so much, though we still don't have anything nice to eat. Apart from the treats William gets us. William always has something nice. Mummy has met William a few times. I think they are quite good friends.

The American soldiers are having a party for us today. I can't wait to go. Last time they had peanut butter. It's delicious. I hope they have ice cream and fruit as well.

"Mummy, hurry up," I run up the stairs and pull on Mummy's sleeve. "What's that?"

"Perfume. William bought it for me. Doesn't it smell nice?"

"Can I have some?" I giggle and then we are hurrying down the stairs and out the door.

As we make our way to the party, I glance at Mummy. She looks much better now. My proper mummy is back at last. She looks very pretty today. I think she's got her best dress on. She turns and smiles at me and we hold hands, our arms swinging back and forth as excited screams and shouts grow nearer and nearer. People are everywhere. I run forward, in and out of the crowd, my heart thudding. I can't stop smiling and then I see him.

"William!"

"Hey there, it's little Anne," he picks me up and swings me round, "where's your mom?"

"She's back there somewhere. Look, here she comes."

William puts me down. He stands there, his green eyes twinkling and his huge smile showing off his perfect teeth. I look to Mummy. She is blushing and she starts to giggle. William takes her hand and kisses it. I think I'm going to be sick. I can't watch anymore. My legs are running, pushing me on in the direction of home.

Grass tickles my leg and I find myself at the back of our house. I push the door and my feet thud up the stairs. I throw myself on my bed and cuddle teddy.

How could she? William's my friend. I saw him first. I think he likes Mummy best now. He gave her some nail polish last week. I close my eyes and rock myself to sleep. Maybe I'll dream of Daddy. Daddy will make everything better.

***

Mummy and me don't talk about William anymore. I haven't seen him since the party a week ago. I don't think I like him now.

I'm going to stay with Peter and Mrs Edwards tonight. Mummy is going to a club. She says she is going to dance and dance. I wish I could go, but she said it's for grown-ups.

After tea I kiss Mummy goodbye and walk down the steps. I turn back to look at her, but she has already closed the door. I gulp. I won't cry.

Mrs Edwards gives me a big hug and I don't feel like crying anymore. I place teddy on the bed and smile. Mrs Edwards is going to read us a story before bed.

Someone is at the window. I can hear them tapping. I pull the curtain back. It's just a branch blowing in the wind. I see something else. It's Mummy. She is walking down the road. Someone is with her. They are holding hands. It's William. They stop and kiss. I turn away and Mrs Edwards is there.

I run to her and she wraps her arms around me.

"It's all right, Anne."

I pull back. "You knew, didn't you?"

"I can't say I'm happy about it, Anne, but your mother has been through a lot."

"I thought she loved my daddy."

"She did. She does. She'll always love your dad. But she's happy. William makes her happy. You like William, don't you?"

"No, I hate him! Mummy doesn't need anyone else. She's got me. Why doesn't she love me anymore?"

"Of course she loves you. Come here. That's it, Anne. Have a good cry. Let it out. Let it all out."

I put my head on the pillow and she strokes my hair. I feel so tired.

***

Mummy is smiling when I see her the next morning. I didn't think I had any tears left, but I can't stop them running down my cheeks.

"Anne, what's wrong?"

Mummy puts her hand on my shoulder.

"I saw you kiss William. And you kissed him like you used to kiss Daddy."

"I'm sorry, Anne. I should have told you. Your daddy is very special. I'll never forget him, but he's not coming back. I didn't mean to fall in love with William."

"Do you love him as much as Daddy?"

"No, Anne," Mummy says forcefully. "No one will ever replace your daddy. But William is a very nice man. He's very fond of me and I'm fond of him. And he has a lot to offer. He owns a chain of restaurants in New York. He's got a nice house and he'll look after us."

"I don't want to live in America. I want to stay here."

"You'll love America, Anne. We can put everything behind us."

"I don't want to put Daddy behind me."

I can't take any more and I run out the house and across the fields. But this time, I'm not going to the camp. I'll never go there again. I run and run and run. Why did you have to leave us, Daddy? We were happy, the three of us. You promised me you would come home.

I stop. William is walking across the field.

"Leave us alone," I am running again. He shan't

catch me.

But I am wrong. He holds my shoulders and stares into my eyes.

"What's wrong, little Anne?"

"You! What do you want with us? We're not going to live in America."

I am fighting him, wriggling to be free. William lets me go and I fall to the ground. I look up into William's eyes. He looks sad.

"I'm sorry, Anne, I never meant to hurt you or your mom," he shrugs his shoulders, "goodbye, Anne. Take care of yourself."

I watch him as he makes for our house. His head is hanging down and his arms are by his side. Something is wrong. I want to run to Mummy and tell her to be careful. But I can't. I have to wait.

I go down by the river and watch it swirling round and round, the wind building and creating rapid ripples. The fish dart in and out of reeds and I'm sure I saw a snake down there too. I don't like snakes.

I can't wait any longer. I have to go home. Rain starts to stab my eyes and my hair is plastered to my face. I have to get to Mummy. I have to save her. But from what, I don't know.

"Mummy? Mummy!" I reach the house.

Silence. I run to the stairs and take two at a time. I don't knock and I burst my way through the door. Mummy is sick. She is holding her tummy and rocking from side to side.

"Anne," she holds out her hand.

"What did William do to you?"

Mummy starts to cry. "Nothing. Nothing, Anne.

He just came to say goodbye."

"Goodbye? He said goodbye to me too. He's not coming back, is he?"

"No, Anne. They're leaving. All of them. They're going home to America."

I am so happy. It is me and Mummy again. Just the two of us. And Daddy. We shan't ever forget Daddy.

My happiness fades. Mummy opens her mouth and I know what she is going to say. We're going to America too.

"He lied, Anne. He lied to me. He said he wanted to marry me, but it was lies, all lies," her voice is a whisper.

"We're not going to America, then?"

"No, Anne. He doesn't own a fancy chain of restaurants. He owns a peanut stall. And he's already got a wife in America."

I stare at Mummy. I put my arms around her and stroke her hair. I am the grown up and she is the child. I tell her it will be all right, but I don't believe what I am saying.

***

Mummy has been very ill since that day. She says she is all right, but she can't face much to eat and she is always being sick. I'm glad William has gone. I don't miss him at all. Peter does. He misses them all. But it's all right for him. His daddy has come home.

Mummy is being very quiet today. I walk down the stairs and peer round the door. She is sitting at the kitchen table reading a letter. It falls to the floor and she is screaming. Mummy is going mad again. I run forward.

"Mummy, are you all right? Have you gone mad again?"

She laughs, a funny giggle. "I don't think so, Anne. No, strangely enough I feel very sane."

She holds my hands and takes a deep breath before continuing. "They've found Daddy."

Mummy *has* gone mad again.

"Your daddy was a prisoner of war in Malaya. They didn't know. But they've found him now and he's coming home."

The room is spinning. Mummy looks funny. Her pale face and blue dress merge together. Suddenly, it is dark. I can remember nothing more.

***

When my eyes open, I find myself in bed. Mummy is dabbing my forehead with a cold cloth. I smile at her, but she is crying.

"Is Daddy really coming home? Is Daddy really alive? Is everything going to be all right?"

Mummy nods her head, but her sobbing becomes louder.

"Don't you want Daddy to come home? Is it because you love William?"

"No, Anne. I didn't ever love William. I just missed your daddy and William offered me companionship, that's all. I love your daddy, Anne."

"Then why are you crying?"

Mummy pulls her cardigan back and pats her tummy. I stare at it. It is big and swollen.

"Mummy, why is your tummy like that?" I'm not sure I want her to answer.

"Because I'm going to have a baby," Mummy blurts out.

"So I'm going to have a brother or sister? That's great. I want a sister. Daddy will be so happy when he comes home," I smile, thinking of my beautiful baby sister.

"You don't understand. No one understands," Mummy is shouting and she runs from the room.

I hear her bedroom door slam. I can't hear her any more, but I know she's crying. I lie back against the pillow. I hope Mummy isn't going to stay with the special people again. I close my eyes and I can't help but smile. My daddy is coming home.

***

I'm scared. Daddy is coming home today. I get up from my bed and walk to the window. I stare at the fields and the grass waving back at me in the wind.

I saw Mr Edwards last week. He used to crack jokes all the time and he was quite handsome, but he isn't anymore. He has horrible scars and he walks with a stick. And he looks so sad. Mummy says it's because war is horrible. She says war does terrible things to men.

Mummy knocks on the door and comes in. She smiles, but I can see the fear in her eyes.

Suddenly, everything goes mad. Daddy is here, shouting up the stairs. He pounds up them and stands at the top. Mummy won't look at him. I barge past her and stare at my daddy. He looks so old. And he looks sad. A tear threatens to fall down my cheek. I want my daddy back. My real daddy.

He breaks into a smile. Perhaps my real daddy is here after all. He throws his arms wide and I run to him, his princess once more.

I feel him stiffen and he pulls away. Mummy is walking towards him. He stares at her tummy. He frowns, then he laughs. Now he is angry.

"Anne, go next door and see Peter. Now!" Daddy snaps.

***

I have been at Peter's for a long time. I fiddle with a little car Mr Edwards made for Peter. I stare at the wall, my hands gripping the wooden toy. My knuckles are white as I try not to throw it at the wall and watch as it smashes into hundreds of pieces.

Mrs Edwards peers round the corner.

"There's someone to see you, love," she smiles.

Daddy walks through the door.

"Come on, Peter, let's leave them alone a minute," Mrs Edwards says.

"Why?" Peter pouts.

Mrs Edwards grips his arm and hauls him to his feet. Daddy and me are alone. He is leaving us. I know he is.

"Anne," he takes a step forward and grasps my hand.

"Don't leave us, Daddy. Please!" my hands are round his waist and I won't let go.

"I'm not going anywhere, Anne. I'm staying right here with you and Mummy."

"You are?"

"Yes."

"What about the baby?" I don't know why the baby matters, but it does.

"The baby will stay with us too. We're a family again, Anne. Lots of things have happened during this war, but none of them matter now. It's all over. Nothing is going to come between us again."

I can't stop smiling. I take Daddy's hand. My daddy has come home for good.

Operation Flora

No one understood how lonely it was being stuck up a tree all on your own. Flora sighed and fluttered her wings. One wing barely moved and the other nearly fell off. Her nose was feeling a bit delicate too and the lacy trim on her dress was a little wonky. She was sure fairies weren't supposed to have problems like this.

She leaned forward, swaying slightly. It was such a long way down. Why did they need such a great big tree? It was only a tiny flat after all. And if they were going to have such a huge tree, then why didn't they decorate it properly? A bit of gold tinsel and five baubles could hardly be called decorating.

But she couldn't really expect anything else of them – well, *her* anyway. Not after her reaction to Flora when she had been presented to them.

Little Damien had been so proud of all his hard work. He had spent hours cutting, colouring, sticking, gluing and glittering. His teacher had called her a masterpiece.

"I'm going to call her Flora and I'm going to give her to my favourite uncle. Well, my only uncle, actually. He's called Uncle Jamie. I'm not going to give her to Aunt Alice though. Mum says she's a miserable old cow."

Flora had tried not to giggle. Surely Alice couldn't be that bad?

"What on earth is that?" Alice said, snorting and

pursing her thin lips.

Flora sighed. It looked like she could be.

"Well, I think she's wonderful. I'm going to place her straight on top of the tree when we get one," Jamie said.

"I am not having a tree on my cream carpet," Alice said, shuddering.

Flora didn't think people had red eyes but Alice's definitely looked red. Scarlet even. Flora had looked at Damien, willing for him to change his mind and keep her.

"Uncle Jamie, you will take good care of Flora, won't you?"

"Of course. How about you come with us and choose a Christmas tree right now? Then you can put Flora on the top," Jamie beamed round the room.

Flora was sure she could see smoke shooting out of Alice's ears.

When they all came trudging back home a few hours later, Alice holding a small bag containing the tinsel and baubles in a vice like grip, Jamie struggling under the weight of the tree and Damien with a huge grin on his face, Flora couldn't help but smile.

She had been pleased at first, especially when Jamie lifted her onto the top of the tree. When the 'decorating' had taken place, all thirty seconds of it and under the supervision of a chilling glare, Flora realised how ridiculous her situation was. It wouldn't have been so bad if she'd had some friends to talk to – a Father Christmas or a snowman. It wasn't much to ask. But tinsel and baubles didn't do a lot. They just sat there all shiny and looking pretty. Besides, they were miles away, right at the bottom.

When Damien had left, Flora thought Alice was going to go wild and slice the tree in two just by looking at it.

"Do you realise how cross I am?" Alice said, slamming the door behind Damien and his mother, who had come to collect her son and been late as usual.

"Yes," Jamie said, easing himself into the armchair and placing his hands behind his head.

"Look at her. Look at that hideous thing he calls a fairy. It all started with her."

Flora had blushed, her wings curling under the piercing stare.

"Her hair is made of string. Blue string. Who ever heard of a fairy with blue hair? And it's falling off. She's only got two strands left."

A tear fell down Flora's cheek. She brushed it away with a wing, wincing as a smattering of glitter glided down to the branches below. She had never felt so unwanted and unloved.

"Well, I think she looks fantastic," Jamie said.

Flora smiled. He thought she was fantastic. Someone cared.

"And why did you let him pick such an enormous…No, that's not the right word. Colossal. Yes, that's it. Look at all those needles on my carpet. Look!"

"Actually, it's my carpet. You moved in with me, but that's not important. What is important are decorations. I think we ought to buy a few more.

How about some lights? All colours of the rainbow. It might brighten up this room a bit."

"My magnolia walls do not need brightening up with disco lights."

Flora watched Alice's face flush from pink, to purple, then red, easing back to pink again. Flora had never seen anyone explode before. She wondered if she was about to. She almost felt disappointed when Alice didn't explode and chose to stomp across the room and slam the door behind her instead.

That had been a week ago. A whole week of loneliness. Flora wasn't sure if she could bear much more. Her hopes were raised when Damien came over at the weekend with some chocolate reindeer to put on the tree. Jamie helped Damien to put one on the next branch down. Flora clapped her wings in delight until ten minutes later, Damien asked Jamie if he could eat them all instead.

Alice was horrified when she came home from her mother's. "You let him eat ten chocolates? At once? What will his mother say? Oh, of course. She won't care, will she? Do you realise how many calories there are in chocolate? Not to mention the amount of sugar."

"He's a child, Alice. Children eat chocolate. A few chocolates won't hurt him. It's Christmas. Anyway, I thought we would be doing you a favour. Perhaps we should have left them on the tree," Jamie said, winking at Damien.

"You put those tacky things on the tree? This tree? That's worse than the fairy."

Flora frowned.

74

"What's wrong with my fairy?" Damien asked, sounding hurt.

"Nothing. I'm sure you did your best, but…um…" Alice said.

"What's wrong with my fairy, Uncle Jamie? Why doesn't Aunt Alice like her?"

"Excuse me, I have to go somewhere," Alice said and she ran from the room.

Jamie knelt down and held Damien's hands. The little boy's eyes filled with tears. Flora could hardly bear to watch and her own eyes glistened.

"Do you know something, Damien? Aunt Alice sometimes gets a bit silly. I think it's something women do every now and then."

Flora tutted.

Jamie continued, "But I've been thinking. I need your help with a very special assignment. It's called Operation Flora. I can't do it on my own. Do you think you can help me?"

Damien grinned and puffed out his chest with pride. Flora watched them leave the room and hung her head. Operation Flora? She wasn't sure she liked the sound of that.

Two hours later and there was still no sign of Alice. There had been a lot more slamming, followed by muttering and banging, then some more slamming and then nothing. And all Flora could hear from Jamie and Damien were muffled voices and squeals of delight. It was awful waiting, just sitting there and waiting for Operation Flora to begin.

Suddenly the door burst open and Damien dashed into the room giggling madly. He ran up to the tree and looked straight at Flora.

"Uncle Jamie said you looked a bit lonely up there all on your own, so I've made you some friends,' Damien said, 'I hope you like them."

Flora looked down at Damien's arms brimming with cotton wool snowmen, tissue paper Father Christmases, cardboard robins, toilet-roll elves and foil stars. Damien licked his lips in concentration and started dangling the decorations over the branches. Flora's heart surged with joy. She had some friends at last. A tear of happiness fell down her cheek. She would never be lonely again.

"Uncle Jamie, hurry up. I can't reach the high branches. I think Flora would like a Father Christmas to talk to. Or maybe she would like a snowman."

Jamie entered the room.

"She can have them all. You've done enough to fill the whole tree," Jamie said, a catch to his voice.

"What's wrong, Uncle Jamie? Don't you like them? Or is it Aunt Alice? She'll go really mad when she sees these, won't she?"

"I love them, Damien. Each and every one of them. And it doesn't matter what Aunt Alice thinks. She won't be seeing them anyway."

"Not at all?"

"No, Damien, she's gone. She's packed her bags and gone."

"Are you sad, Uncle Jamie? Won't you be really lonely?"

Jamie looked at Damien. Then he smiled, a huge beaming smile.

"Actually, I don't feel very sad at all. I think it's

something that should have happened a long time ago. And you're coming to stay with me for a week after Christmas, so I shan't even be a tiny bit lonely. Come on, let's finish the tree," Jamie said, placing an elf an inch away from Flora. "Look at Flora's face, Damien. She looks so happy. I rather think Operation Flora has been a success."

A Walk in the Park

"Wow! Just look at it," Sarah cried, unable to believe her eyes. She looked about her, marvelling at the beauty of the ancient buildings and the cute little side shops, which had sprung up over the years. Then she looked down at the two children at her side, wrapped up snugly in anoraks, hats and gloves.

It had been years since she had visited the town. She remembered the fun she'd had as a young girl; the excitement felt as she carefully chose from the myriad of jars of succulent sweets in the corner shop and the joy she had experienced from throwing chunks of bread to the ducks in the park nearby.

A frown creased her forehead as she recalled the tears and goodbyes when she had left. Her eyes were still on Charlie and Beth, each clasping the other's hands. It had been the right decision. She wouldn't have wanted it any other way.

Her thoughts were interrupted by a cry from her young son. "Mum, it's so cold here. I want to go home. It's warmer there."

"Come on, love, it's not for long. You know I wanted to come back and see the town where I grew up. We'll go home soon, I promise. Let's buy some bread and feed the ducks. I used to enjoy that when I was a little girl."

This offer seemed to please the small boy and he ran on, dragging his sister with him. They reached the park, the children darting ahead, excited at the prospect of seeing the ducks.

Sarah smiled, enjoying the view. It hadn't changed that much. The tall trees were still there, blowing gracefully in the wind as the river continued to meander by. People still flocked there, whatever the weather, dogs on leads dragging owners or mothers with children, attempting to tire them out, on the swings and roundabouts, their excited squeals filling the air. Couples of all ages ambled by and businessmen strode through the park on their way to important meetings, mobile phones clamped to their ears.

Her thoughts became filled with images of a tall, dark figure. She remembered their happy times together, there in that very park. Her mood became gloomy as the man troubled her mind. She had really loved him. Nothing had ever come between them – until she left.

Sarah looked down at the inviting park bench. She sank down onto the wooden seat, her memories taking her back to a time before; she'd sat there, on that same bench, the night before she'd left. He had begged and pleaded with her not to go. He'd been adamant that no good would come of her decision. She knew he had been right in some ways, but she had come to love the way of life out there in Australia and she had her gorgeous children. She wouldn't change that for anything, but she'd had to come back; just for a while. She didn't know if it was to see her old home again or if it was the chance of seeing him that had brought her back.

As she glanced in hope at everyone walking by,

she knew that it was him she wanted to see. She knew he would still come to the park. He had to.

"Mum, we've finished. We've run out of bread. Can we go on the swings now?" Beth asked, her pretty face full of excitement.

Sarah took their hands and held them tight, heading in the direction of the play area. She looked back wistfully at the bench. Why would he come here anyway? she asked herself. She didn't even know where he lived. She had felt so sure he was still there, in their home town, but her thoughts began to waver and now she wasn't so certain.

She had written to him for years after she left, but he'd never replied. He hadn't been a great letter writer anyway, though she had hoped he would try because of his love for her.

She wanted to wait there, in the park, just in case he did come, but the children were starting to tire and shiver with the cold. It was no good; it was time to go. She sighed as they turned in the direction of the exit. Pausing, she looked back over her shoulder.

Panic gripped her. What if he'd already been there? He might have walked by her, neither one able to recognise the other anymore. It had been so long. Would they know each other?

Still, she reasoned, it was too late. She turned back and walked on. She wouldn't see him now. Anyway, what would she achieve if she did? He had been angry with her all those years ago. Would he want to know her now? As thoughts whirled round in her mind, a tear rolled down her cheek.

"Sarah?" a voice from behind.

She spun round, an expression of expectancy on her face. She looked at the man facing her. Was it? No...Yes...

"That must be him," Beth nudged her brother, wide eyed.

Her daughter's words propelled Sarah into action and she made the first move, her grin spreading wider, as did her arms.

The couple clung to each other for some time, tears of happiness trickling down their cheeks. Sarah knew she'd been forgiven. She looked up into the man's face: her beloved twin brother. He was the one she had left behind for a life in a foreign country with the Australian student she'd fallen in love with.

"And what about Mum and Dad? They'd turn in their graves if they knew you were going off with him. He's no good, Sarah."

Well, he'd been right, but she didn't care. She had her brother back and she wasn't going to lose him again.

The Secret Diary of Marvin Martin aged 14 ½

Monday, July 10th

It's over! Today is finally over. But I've got to go through hell tomorrow - all thanks to Mum and her thong. Ugh! I still feel sick thinking about it. Thongs look good on women like Taylor Swift, not Maureen Martin. Mum must be at least twenty years older and twenty stone heavier.
I thought she wore big knickers. There's usually a row of them on the washing line. Like great gigantic grey pillowcases, they are. Well, today of all days she seems to have discovered thongs. It wouldn't have been so bad if she had worn a white one. Well, on Mum it would have been as bad, but to make things even worse, she wore a black one – with white trousers. I'd have forgiven Taylor Swift that but not Mum. And not in front of Stuart Biggs.
They're against me. All of them. I'm sure of it. Mum. Stuart. Miss Sawyer. She knows Stuart hates me. He's the cleverest in the class and he's good-looking too. Like all his friends. So why on earth she put us together for that science project is beyond me. Stuart was pretty horrified at the idea as well, though not as horrified as when Miss Sawyer said we would need to get together after school. And certainly not as horrified as when he walked into our kitchen and Mum was bending over to get

her homemade 'break-a-tooth' buns out the oven. Stuart swore blind she farted too. But I know it was the dodgy floorboard. Our house is ancient. Dodgy floorboards everywhere. Stuart wouldn't have it and was texting everyone about it as he left.

I wouldn't have felt so awful if Stuart's mum was a hideous old bag too, but she's a goddess. Even better than Taylor. And that's saying something.

Stuart won't be able to put his phone down tonight. Dad would have had to come home at the exact moment Stuart was leaving. Stuart's dad has got a Mercedes. My dad's got a scooter. With a girly basket on the front. I didn't need to see Stuart's face. I knew the smirk was there. But he turned round anyway, just so I could see it.

Though I must admit that smirk went pretty quickly when his mum turned up in her bright pink Beetle. She gave me a big kiss on the cheek, which was rather nice. I wonder how long lipstick marks stay on if you don't wash. And then she squeezed; yes, I must write it again, *squeezed* Stuart's cheek and called him, 'sweetie'.

Perhaps tomorrow won't be so bad after all.

The Lover

Nigel watched as the naked woman writhed on top of him, her bulging breasts bouncing in time to Vivaldi's Four Seasons. She licked her Ferrari red lips and a mischievous grin settled on her youthful face.

Nigel's breathing quickened as she arched her back like an Olympic gymnast and grabbed her sheer black stockings. As she leaned forward to bind his wrists to the bedstead, he groaned with pleasure. She smiled, drawing a lethal-looking nail down his chest. He flinched and she laughed. His nervous laughter joined hers as she went back to her bouncing, though it wasn't long before he could barely remember his name as she performed tricks he hadn't even dreamt of.

Twenty minutes later, it was all over. Nigel lay back against the satin sheets, his breathing hard and fast. A grin was fixed on his face and he reached for his cigarette packet. He lit up, enjoying the soothing smoke as it burst into his lungs. He coughed. He coughed again, choking this time. His hands clawed at the bedside table. Petrified, he put the Ventolin inhaler to his mouth. This wasn't how it happened in the movies. The hero was never wheezy and the woman always stayed, stroking the hero's manly chest.

Nigel sighed. Once she'd bagged her money, she had practically run from the room. Perhaps if he had asked her name she would have stayed. Still, he'd

84

got what he wanted and he didn't always have to pay for it. No, he could have anyone he wanted.

He thought about Stacey. He hadn't had to give her a penny. She was beautiful, with long, lithe legs and thick blonde hair, which framed her elegant heart-shaped face. Her skin had been as pale as porcelain and as flawless. He had spent hours just gazing at that face. They made a handsome couple, both tall and good-looking.

A few years had passed since he had seen Stacey, but he knew he looked just as good.

His mornings at the gym kept him trim and the sun beds made him look like he had just stepped off a beach in the Bahamas. A frown marred his features. Stacey had almost been his downfall. He hadn't meant to fall for her. It had started like all the others – in the bedroom. She was a fantastic lover, but there was more to it than that. She had been so tender, clever and fun to be with.

When he realised he was in love with her, he had been willing to change his whole life. He would have given up everything for her. But she didn't want him. She never had.

Another woman took over, quashing Stacey's perfect image. Noreen. He gathered his clothes together, thinking how lucky he was that Noreen didn't care for their city house. No, the little wife was safely tucked away in their Berkshire home.

He knew he was beastly to her. He just couldn't help it. It didn't matter anyway. She always came back for more. She had even stuck by him when the Stacey affair had erupted. Despite it all, she was at home now, keeping the house spotless in case the

Queen came to visit. Nigel sniggered, pleased at his little joke. It kept her busy, he supposed and out of his business.

Thinking of business, he knew he ought to be getting back to work. It was going to be a long meeting that afternoon. At least it would be colourful. He grinned. Everyone was going to be there, so there would be several outbursts, at least one caused by him. He made for the bathroom and stopped by the window.

He savoured the smell of spring. The sun was shining and the daffodils were displaying their vivid yellow, giving a hint of things to come over the months ahead. His gaze came to rest on the bench by the brook.

It was Noreen who had fallen in love with the brook. They had been married for three months and Nigel had just got his first appointment in the city. He knew they couldn't afford it, but he hadn't been quick enough getting rid of the estate agent's details.

He remembered Noreen stroking the photograph, her small fingers caressing it lovingly. He had taken her to see it, thinking she would hate its vastness, the huge rooms and dark décor. It was the garden that had swung it. The brook and the myriad of flowers cascading like waterfalls down the lawn slopes. She had loved the old statues and ivy walkways. Fool that he was, he had still loved her then, so the house was hers.

She went off the house rather rapidly when she found him in bed with Stacey. She hadn't set foot in it since.

Stacey got what she wanted when she sold her story to the papers. Somehow she even managed to get a book deal, so she had more than her five minutes of fame.

Nigel pulled away from the window and entered the bathroom. He splashed cold water onto his face. He hadn't been able to believe it when Noreen stayed with him. She coped with journalists camped out on their doorstep, funny phone calls and everyone pitying her.

Nigel closed his eyes and twelve years fell away to their wedding day. They say every bride looks beautiful and Noreen was no exception. Her normally dull, dark hair was shiny and silky in a French pleat and her usually plain face was carefully made-up. His mother said she looked like a princess. On that day, Nigel had to agree. The dress was white, reflecting the virgin that she was, nipped in to show off her tiny waist and billowing out to the ground. Her cat-green eyes had held his, full of love and hope for their future. His blue ones had drowned in hers, mirroring the same dreams.

It was all Noreen's fault that everything had gone wrong. He had put up with her insisting she remain a virgin until their wedding day. If he had known what a flop she would be in the bedroom, it would have saved her parents a fortune.

He often wondered why he stayed with her. It wasn't as if they'd had children. He shuddered at the thought. He hadn't even wanted a child with Stacey. Besides, children were annoying, smelly things.

Ruefully, he looked at his reflection in the

mirror. It hadn't done his career any harm to be married to the Police Commissioner's daughter. Noreen was also good to have around. There was no one like Noreen when it came to impressing guests. If he snapped his fingers, she was there within seconds and she would put Nigella Lawson in the shade when it came to cooking. Add to that the fact he only went home to her at the weekends and his life wasn't so bad.

Nigel pulled his trousers on, a smirk playing at the corner of his lips. He wondered what Noreen had been doing while he had been cavorting with the gorgeous blonde. He could picture her in the kitchen, kneading pastry. He cringed. She was only slight, but she had very strong hands. He had found that out on their wedding night.

Now she was putting the pastry aside, walking round to the sink, in her polka dot dress, like Julia Roberts in Pretty Woman. He had told her enough times it was old hat, but she seemed to wear it more often after that. Perhaps the dozy cow was waiting for Richard Gere to arrive in a white limo, a red rose between his teeth. Nigel scoffed. The closest she got to a man at the door was the postman.

He pushed his feet into his shoes, a pang of guilt tweaking at him. Poor Noreen. She had tried her best, but a man had needs. He thought about the blonde and grinned.

***

The striking blonde leaned back against the fading taxi seats. She was shaking as she lit a cigarette.

"No smoking, love," the cabby yelled.

She stamped on the offending weed, imagining it was Nigel's face. She scratched at her arms, then her legs and stomach. Every part of her body was crawling – crawling with his vile touch. She knew she should have stayed longer. After all, she had been paid to. She just hoped she wasn't found out.

***

Nigel closed the bathroom door behind him and made his way downstairs. He grabbed his brief case. It was a shame all good things had to come to an end.

***

At the exact moment Nigel found himself bound with stockings, pastry had been the last thing on Noreen's mind. She had been sitting at the kitchen table. Papers and ledgers were strewn across the shiny surface. A frown creased her brow as she stared at the figures on the bank statement. It was the huge debit from their joint account that caused her concern. She looked at her watch and the frown eased.

***

Nigel paused at the front door. He had forgotten something. Ah, his laptop. He turned and walked towards the lounge.

The bomb detonated, ripping through every brick

and edifice of the house. The once solid structure was reduced to rubble in seconds. The terrorist group, Al Sneneda stepped forward to claim credit for the atrocity. The media and newspapers were in a frenzy. Westminster mourned the loss of a key minister.

***

In their Berkshire home, Noreen was still settled at the kitchen table. The huge deficit would leave her a little short for a while, but it was worth every penny. Besides, she would more than quadruple that when the insurance money came through.

The Dark Place

I hate this dark place. A cobweb gently glides over my cheek, its maker long gone, searching for fresh food. A squeak in the corner reminds me that I am not alone. The rats have been my only friends for the past few weeks. We used to fight each other for food, but food no longer interests me.

I jump, startled by the sudden wailing in the corridor. It is the same every night, but my senses still fear her. I smile, her incoherent babbling highlighting her madness. I thought I, too, would succumb to the dementia. I have no such joy. I have to live with my fate every single moment of every day.

The hours tick by, tick-tock, tick-tock. I have no idea of time, but the growing light warns me that daybreak is dawning. The birds launch into song, mocking me, crowing at me. They know today is the day, my very last on this earth.

I wonder if the reprieve will come. I wonder if I want it to. Or will my death be a welcome respite from the pain I endure minute by minute, hour by hour? I imagine my solicitors, pouring over the huge volumes of law, searching for the slightest glimmer of hope. They shan't find it. Of that, I am certain. What good would it do anyway? Too many wish me dead. Too many want me to pay for my crime.

Tomorrow life will go on. In a day or two I will

be forgotten, just another number in a long line of statistics. But not everyone will forget me.

"Mummy, don't leave me. Mummy! Please," her frightened cries tore into my soul, my wrists bound and my body dragged away to the car.

I long to see her, even just once more. I want to touch her face, the rosy cheeks, the rosebud mouth. My fingers want to wind round her long, blonde hair and my lips kiss her forehead.

I shall never forget that last look: the quivering lips, the tear-streaked face and sunken shoulders. Her whole world had collapsed around her. It would never be the same again.

I have to go on. I must, for her sake. I wonder where she is. Maybe she is crying, all alone with no one to care for her. I wipe away my own tears. Crying won't help her. I should have thought of that before I picked up the knife.

But he deserved it. I feel no remorse, no sorrow for the blood he shed. It was that final blow to her head that did it. No longer could I stand by, my silence making me as bad as he. My previous interference had only led him to bestow the same punishment upon me. There had been only one way out and I had taken that path. I had to save my munchkin, my Millie. She is safe now; he can harm no other mortal.

"Ella," it is a whisper.

I turn round. They are here already. Silence greets me. Just the wind whistling through the hollows.

I can almost see the noose before me, dancing its merry jig. I stroke my neck, sure I can feel the rough rope tight against my neck. I gag, the bile catching in my throat. I can't do this. I can't. My fingers claw at the floor, my jagged nails screeching in my ears.

The brightening rays sting my eyes. I wonder how many other poor souls will follow in my footsteps, waking to a sunny day, its shimmering brilliance to be marred by death. Their death.

The campaigning has been going on for years. So many want to change the law, but they can't save me. It is all too late for me.

My head swings round. My jailors have come for me. Even they look sickened as they motion me forward. My pupils battle against the stabbing light as I at last see the sun. My limbs aching and my body stiff, I force one foot in front of the other. I hold my head high.

I am almost there now. Shouts greet my ears. The crowds are heaving.

"Ella! Ella!" they chant. "Free Ella!"

I smile. The campaign will go on.

I take my place and wait for the darkness to envelop me before the final act. I say a last prayer for my child and one for the future. Maybe after today, the gallows will come down for good.

Home

Six o' clock in the morning. Another day Muriel would rather be dead. She opened her eyes and closed them again. Anne would be here soon. She tried not to cry, but Anne always made her cry.

***

Anne's soft-soled shoes squeaked on the shiny surface of the floor. She looked at her watch. Six o' clock. Another dreadful day to spend washing wrinkly skin, wiping sagging bottoms and changing one hideous floral outfit for another equally hideous floral outfit. She pushed the door open. Muriel. It was always Muriel first. Get the worst one over and done with. That had always been her motto.

***

Muriel heard the hinges heave. Anne was there, standing and watching. Muriel didn't need to open her eyes to see the spiky black hair and surly smile. The beady black eyes would narrow soon and then she would spring forward, her hands hauling Muriel upwards. Muriel stayed as still as she could. If she were still enough, perhaps Anne would think she was dead. Perhaps if she wished hard enough, she would be.

***

Anne stared at the still figure. She shook her head and sighed. Stupid old biddy. All of them were stupid old biddies, but Muriel was the worst. She had diabetes and she was riddled with arthritis, but nothing was supposed to be wrong with her brain. Anne knew different.

"Wakey, wakey time, Muriel," Anne said, leaping towards the bed.

***

Muriel bristled. She held her breath, waiting for the pinch of fingers, the vile language to be unleashed and the stale breath to blast into her ear. She wasn't disappointed.

***

Anne slammed the door shut behind her. Thank goodness that was over. A smirk settled on her lips. Repulsive. That's what Muriel was, with her varicose veins and bedsores bulging. Ugh. She often wondered how she stood the job. Though someone had to do it. And she, Anne, put herself through it each and every day. Her mother had found her the job and told her that Anne would make the perfect carer. Her mum was so proud of her. Anne's smile slipped. Poor Mum hadn't been so well lately. She wouldn't take herself off to the doctors, either. It was beginning to be a bit of a worry.

***

Muriel sat staring out the window and let the tears fall. Her breathing was shallow as soft wheezes wrestled to be let out. Slowly, her breathing became easier. Why did Anne treat her so terribly? Did Anne not think she herself would get old? Was her body not going to breakdown, bit by bit? Would she not one day face the prospect of being placed in a home? Perhaps she thought Muriel had always been old, that Muriel had never been young.

Muriel looked at the photographs depicting her son and daughters, her grandson and granddaughters. Was Muriel too hideous to have ever been in love? To have gotten married and borne beautiful children? Maybe Anne ignored it. The residents of the care home weren't people to her, just objects she was paid to do something with.

***

"Anne, there's a phone call for you," Debbie said, putting her hand on Anne's shoulder, "I'll see to Violet."

"Who on earth would be ringing me this early?" Anne asked, staring at her older colleague.

"I've no idea. Go on, get and answer it and then you'll know," Debbie said, whirling Anne round in the direction of the office.

Anne frowned. It was her mum. She just knew it.

***

Muriel leaned back, wriggling around in the hard chair. She and Harry had often joked about care homes. Neither had thought they would ever end up in one. Not that her Harry had. Muriel thought about the cancer. First prostate, then bowel, followed by the stomach. She shivered. Poor Harry. But she had nursed him. Been there for him and watched him slowly slip away with each passing day.

Now it was her turn. She remembered the fight she'd had with her children.

"Come and live with us, Mum," her eldest daughter had said.

"Your place is too small. We've bags of room," the youngest daughter this time.

"I'm a bachelor. I throw all my clothes on the floor, never do any washing up and I don't even own a Hoover. You'd hate it, Mum," her son said.

Muriel couldn't argue with that. But she wouldn't have wanted to live with any of them. She hadn't had children so they would look after her in her old age. She wanted them to live their own lives.

"None of you need worry. I'm going into a care home. It's all sorted out, just come and visit me now and then, that's all I ask," Muriel announced.

She had watched every face, seen the shock register and stay.

"But you always said you didn't want to go into a home," her eldest daughter was the first to recover.

"I know I did, but I've got to face facts. I'm not getting any younger. My body is beginning to let me down and I need help."

"You're not going into a home," her son had said, starting the argument.

She had won it eventually but at what cost? Muriel looked at a photograph of Harry. Why couldn't she have gone with him? Why did she have to wait another ten years? Maybe more. More years of Anne. More years of her body becoming increasingly useless. Perhaps her mind would be next. Then she wouldn't know what Anne was doing to her anymore. Her mind might allow her to retreat, to relive her life with Harry. She closed her eyes. Oh, Harry.

***

"What on earth's the matter, Anne?" Debbie asked, throwing the half dozen dirty towels in her arms to the floor and hurrying to hug Anne.

"Mum's had a stroke," Anne stammered.

"Lots of people recover from strokes. She'll be all right. Just you wait and see," Debbie said, stroking Anne's arm.

"But she's not old. She's only forty-two. Only old people have strokes," Anne said.

"Strokes can happen to anyone, at any age. You don't have to be old. And we all get old one day. Something happens to get us sooner or later," Debbie said.

Another flurry of tears fell down Anne's face.

Debbie's hands flew to her cheeks. "Me and my big mouth. Look, you get off and see your mum. She'll be all right. Just you wait and see."

***

Anne stood in the driveway and stared up at the care home. It had been four weeks since she had last seen it. And there it was. A huge red brick building, boldly standing there just as before as if nothing had changed. But everything had changed.

Anne smiled. Her mum was doing well. It had only been a slight stroke. Anne had looked after her mum - and her dad, useless to begin with, now knew the drill. Her mum had been awful at first, a real nuisance. Stubborn one minute, angry the next. Then tearful. Just like the old people at the home. But her mum couldn't be like them. She and her mum went shopping, drank wine at the weekend and watched all the soaps together. Her mum did all Anne's washing and ironing. She cooked and cleaned. Her mum was supposed to look after her, not the other way round.

But those four weeks had taught Anne a lot. And she had remembered Debbie's words. Debbie was right. Everyone got old one day. Her mum was getting older, as was her Dad and Anne herself. She'd just taken each day for granted, but every day they were getting older. Everyone in the care home was old, though they hadn't always been that way. They'd been young once – just like her, with their lives before them.

Anne took a step closer to the home. It was good to be back. The first thing she was going to do was to go and see Muriel. She had something she wanted to say to her.

Anne knocked at the door. Nothing. Perhaps it was just because she hadn't knocked before; she usually marched straight in. She opened the door and peeked in. Muriel wasn't there. Neither were the photographs on the bedside table or the pile of soggy tissues ready for the bin. There was just a bed, with the sheets just so, waiting to welcome a new resident and furniture ready to be filled with the last belongings of another who needed care.

"It's great to have you back," Debbie said, coming into the room.

"Where's Muriel?" Anne asked, already knowing the answer.

"Poor love. She passed away last week."

"But I didn't say sorry. I didn't get to tell her how very sorry I am," Anne said, her face in her hands.

"Sorry for what?"

Anne didn't reply. She stood there, unaware of the shrug of shoulders and of the door closing softly and feet fading into the distance.

It was a while before she stopped crying, a while before she made a decision and a while before a smile came to her face.

It was too late for Muriel. But it wasn't too late for the others.

***

Muriel never knew what happened to Anne. Not that it mattered. For Muriel was very happy, because Harry had come. He'd stood with his arms outstretched. Muriel had gone to him, taken a step with him. And another. At last, she was home.

Spaceman Sam

He couldn't believe his eyes. Surely not right there in the supermarket? He tugged at his mother's sleeve.

"Matthew, I'm talking," she swiped at his arm.

"But, Mum, it's Sam. He's here."

She ignored him, continuing to chat to Mrs Ramsden from number five. "Those boys next door are so noisy. Parents have no idea these days."

Matthew's eyes were drawn back to the figure of Sam. He blinked. Sam was still there. But how could he be? He should be on his spaceship patrolling the universe. Matthew stared at Sam. He was huge, at least ten feet tall. His silver spacesuit sparkled and his helmet was enormous. Light bounced off its shield, dazzling Matthew's eyes. He smiled. Spaceman Sam was actually there, right in front of him and he was walking his way.

Matthew had never seen a spaceman carrying a shopping basket before. But Matthew supposed even spacemen needed to shop somewhere. He had always liked *Bob the Builder* best. That was until Spaceman Sam had come along. The shiny suited man had proceeded to take over his bedroom. Duvet, curtains, lamp; Matthew had it all.

He frowned. He wondered where Sam had parked the spaceship. Sam's spaceship was brilliant. It was the biggest spaceship Matthew had ever seen. Not that he had seen that many up close, or from far away for that matter. But it was big anyway. So where was it? It couldn't be in the car park. That was always full. He knew that because his mother moaned about it every time they came shopping.

Suddenly Sam's spaceship was the last thing on Matthew's mind. The spaceman was bounding towards him, his mighty boots almost as big as Matthew himself. But something wasn't right. It was Colin. Where was Colin? He should have been by Sam's side. Sam was nothing without Colin. They were inseparable. Colin was the first two-headed cat to land on the moon. And in the adventure, 'Planet Colin' he had discovered a brand new planet all by himself.

Matthew hoped Colin was all right. Perhaps he was flying the spaceship. Maybe it was hovering over the supermarket at that very moment. He would have to ask Sam. The spaceman stopped in front of him, his head taller than the highest shelf. Matthew gulped. He opened his mouth. No words came out. Sam bent towards him and a gigantic gloved hand reached out. Matthew's body went rigid from head to toe. Sam patted the boy on the head and he was gone, striding down the aisle.

"Matthew, what on earth is wrong with you?" his mother took his hand, gripping it to stop him shaking.

"Did you see him? Did you see him pat me on the head?"

"What are you talking about?"

"Spaceman Sam. He was here. He touched my head."

His mother swung round. "I can't see anyone,

Matthew."

"Well, he's gone now. But you should have seen him. It was Sam. He's the bestest ever," Matthew's green eyes glazed over.

His mother glared at him. "Matthew, please stop being so rude. I'm having a conversation with Mrs Ramsden. I shan't be long and then we'll go home."

"Can I go after Sam? Can I, Mum? Can I?"

"Matthew!"

His shoulders slumped and he watched his mother's lips twitch as she gabbled on. He tried not to think about Sam, but he couldn't help it. He wondered if Sam was planning a long trip. In the last adventure Sam had saved the world from Evil Eric, the barbarian spaceman. Maybe Sam was going on holiday. He deserved one. He always worked very hard. Matthew wasn't sure where spacemen went on holiday. He hoped Sam was going to Bognor Regis like they were.

Matthew wondered if the supermarket stocked special spacemen provisions. They did have some funny shaped freezers, which contained strange looking food. That had to be it.

He kicked at a piece of paper on the ground. His mother sounded as if she would never stop talking. He wondered if she would notice if he went after Sam. Now she was laughing, giggling about Jilly from number ten and her disastrous perm.

He slowly edged his trainer-clad feet down the aisle, the red reflectors shining brightly. His mother's arms were flapping up and down as she described something and Mrs Ramsden was nodding her head in agreement. His heart hammered and he dived round the corner. He paused and listened.

"And what about Paula's tattoo? It's disgusting."

Matthew grinned. He had done it. Now he had to find Sam. He smiled smugly. He knew just where Sam would be. Rows and rows of freezers stood before him. An old man stooped over one, his balding head as shiny as Sam's suit. Two freezers down, a woman was staring at her shopping list.

The hairs on the back of his neck were rigid. Someone was behind him. Soft breath blew onto his collar. A grunt, a groan, then a giggle. He swung round and two older boys laughed as they ran past.

Matthew turned his attention back to Sam. He started to panic. He couldn't see him anywhere. What if he was too late? What if Sam had already gone? He started to sprint, his small legs pumping up and down.

A glint of silver caught his eye. It was Sam, but he wasn't where he was supposed to be. He was in the forbidden section. What was Sam doing there? His dad loved the forbidden section, but his mum didn't ever let him go near it.

Matthew was sure the butterflies in his stomach were working their way into his throat. He had never been this close to the forbidden section before. There were green bottles, yellow, pink and blue ones too. All the colours of the rainbow were lined up along the shelves. Spaceman Sam picked out some brown bottles. Matthew counted twenty-four of them. Sam must be very thirsty.

What was he doing now? No, he couldn't be. Sam was making his way to the checkout. Matthew hurried forward, his nerves forgotten. He wondered if the supermarket took silver stones. All the shops in space did.

Matthew's chest was on fire as he ran after Sam. It was worse than sports day. He hated running. Skateboarding was much better. But they didn't let you do that at school.

Spaceman Sam paused, perhaps remembering an urgent supply for his mission. Matthew stopped, still fifty yards away. He felt light-headed. He wasn't going to make it.

Why was he bothering anyway? He was going to the Spaceman Sam Live Show later that afternoon. But it wouldn't be the same. He would be surrounded by hundreds and hundreds of screaming kids. His best mate, Danny, would be so impressed if Matthew told him he had talked to Spaceman Sam. He had to do it. He had to find out about Sam's next mission. Everyone would be so jealous.

Sam was on the move again, striding closer and closer to the checkout.

"No!" Matthew said, diving towards the shimmering figure.

Another stood before him, towering over him, threatening to eat him whole.

"Matthew, there you are," his mum stepped towards him. "I told you never to run off like that. Don't you ever do that again. I was so worried."

She reached for him, her arms as long as Mr Tickle wrapping around him. He fought for freedom, his eyes firmly on Sam.

"Let me go."

"What's wrong with you, Matthew? I shan't take

you to see that show if you carry on like that."

He didn't care. He was going to see Sam now, the real Sam. Everyone knew it wasn't really Spaceman Sam in the show. No, the real Sam had far more important things to do.

Matthew looked at his mother and then back to Sam. He hung his head and peered round at his mother once more. Her ice-cold blue eyes stared at him. Grown-ups never understood.

"I'm sorry, Mum, but I have to do this," Matthew said, pushing his mother away and he was gone, flying through the air.

"Wait, Spaceman Sam, wait!" Matthew reached the checkout.

The exit doors sprang open as Sam prepared to go through. He stopped, swivelling round. Then he waved to Matthew and vanished through the doors. Matthew stared after him, his own mission failed.

If Only

I look around at my colleagues with envy.

"Are you okay, Jamilla?" Shirley asks, stopping her filing for a moment and looking straight at me.

I nod my head. Blink a tear away. Force a smile. Shirley starts filing again. How can I tell her? How can I find the words to say how I really feel?

"If I was going on a nice long holiday, I'd be dancing round the room, not looking like someone had nicked my wallet," she says, staring at me again. "Pakistan, eh? I've never even been on a day trip to France. Closest I've got to Pakistan is Portsmouth."

How I would love to go to France. To Portsmouth.

"My Trevor had a big bonus this month. I thought he might whisk me away to Rome or Paris. But no, he's buying a motorbike instead. Another one. I don't know why I put up with him," Shirley says, prodding at a speck of chipped nail polish.

I do. I would put up with Trevor. Shirley doesn't mean her words anyway. I see the way she looks at his photo on her desk, the love lurking beneath her voice when he rings her mobile and the sheer joy in her eyes when he sends flowers to the office.

I look away, see John. Tall. Handsome. Kind. My breath catches in my throat.

"I don't know why you two haven't got it together yet. Anyone can see you're mad about each other," Shirley says, following my gaze.

Another man enters my head. I don't know if he's tall, or handsome or kind. All I have of him is a grainy photograph. But I will know him soon enough. If only life could be different.

Gus

Thank goodness they had gone. Gus stared out the window, gleefully watching the van weave from side to side as it almost buckled under the strain of its large load.

He stepped back, clapped his hands and smiled. He wanted to dance around the room. What was stopping him? Nothing! He launched one foot in front of the other and spun round and round, waving his arms wildly.

His smile slowly faded. He remembered the last time he had danced. Oh dear, oh dear. If anyone wasn't meant to dance, it was he, Gus Williams. He tried to stop. He tottered and teetered, teetered and tottered. And crashed to the floor in a crumpled heap.

Gus lay there a while. No bones broken. Ha ha. Of course there were no broken bones; he was a ghost. But not a very good ghost. Gus sighed. He wasn't actually very good at anything.

He thought about the couple who had just left – his nephew, David, and his wife, Beatrice. Gus was certain he hadn't been dead for more than five minutes before they ran over the threshold and took over his house. He knew they were his only surviving relatives, but surely it wouldn't have hurt them to shed even the tiniest tear for him?

"He always was a stingy old git," were the first words past David's lips as he entered his new home.

"At last I've got something from the old boy, though I can't say it's very nice."

"It's awful. Look at those drab walls. Grey. I detest grey," Beatrice said, dropping to her knees in one swift movement and trailing her skinny finger along the skirting boards. "Mmm, as I thought. Bachelors are useless with dusters."

Gus had swooped down the stairs and opened his mouth to unleash a chilling wail.

"What was that, David? Did you hear a squeak? I can't abide mice."

"It's probably rats," David said.

Beatrice performed a perfect wail. "Right, that's it. I can't stand rats. I'm ringing the exterminator right now," she said, marching over to the telephone.

With slumped shoulders, Gus stumbled back up the stairs to his favourite room. He tried to ease himself through the closed door and stopped. He had done it again. His face was just about through, together with one leg, but the rest of him refused to budge. He gave up and pushed the door open.

For once the sunlit study failed to bring a smile to his face. He opened his mouth wide and poked and prodded about a bit. There was no obvious reason why he was squeaking. He tried again. More of a kitten noise this time. Perhaps if he worked on his technique, he would be sending them packing by the end of the week.

If he could cry, Gus would have had huge, hulking great tears streaming down his face. David said he had never given him anything. What about the lorry he had spent months carving when David was small? And the toy soldiers and games? As David had grown into a teenager, Gus had never forgotten a birthday or Christmas. A parcel had always been sent in the post. Perhaps it hadn't been enough.

Gus knew he hadn't seen David for twenty years, but that wasn't Gus' fault. His sister, God rest her soul, had moved to Australia and Gus wasn't one for flying or any mode of transport for that matter. Even a bicycle made him feel a bit queasy.

How people change, Gus thought. And not always for the better. He shook his head. Nephew or no nephew, Australia would be getting their precious David back sooner than they thought.

Gus worked very hard over the forthcoming months. He made things crash and bang in the middle of the night. It was a shame David used ear plugs and didn't hear a thing, though when he heard the raucous rasps emanating from Beatrice's mouth, he realised why.

He then tried moving furniture around the rooms. Surely that would shock them? It might have, if Gus had been able to move anything. His eight stone frame had never been known for its strength.

Gus watched them slowly take over his home, erasing every memory of him from the house. The study was left until last, but Gus knew it wouldn't be long before his beloved books were binned and the furniture broken down into firewood.

It was the thought of fire that gave Gus his magnificent idea. Every evening, David and Beatrice sat comfortably on the sofa, with mugs of cocoa on the coffee table, as they soaked up the glorious flames of the roaring fire. David would read 'A Hundred and One Ways to be an Ungrateful Bastard' (that wasn't its actual title, but Gus' eyes weren't the best and he was sure it was something along those lines) and Beatrice would knit – usually something in green.

Gus couldn't stop smiling. He could just imagine their faces as he glided down the chimney and emerged from the ferocious flames with his most evil glare.

It should have worked. Getting stuck in the chimney didn't help. Gus had forgotten how narrow it was and he still hadn't mastered the art of sweeping through solid matter.

In the end it was something very simple that had caused the couple to sell up and race rapidly back to the other side of the world. It was a Saturday morning and Gus was just coming out of the study when he collided with David. Well, collided would have been the apt word if Gus hadn't suddenly found that he was able to pass through people at that exact moment. He didn't, however, get quite the response he would have expected. It was more of a laugh, then a groan, followed by a:

"Not you! It is you, isn't it? That's just great. You couldn't just die and be done with it, could you? No, you have to stick around and stay here with us. Well, I'm not staying here with you. You can stick your scummy house."

Gus hadn't hung around to hear the rest. He didn't care. They were leaving! And they had. And now someone else was coming to live in his house. Right now. He could hear their car coming up the drive. It was a Volvo. He liked Volvos. The family hadn't seemed too bad either. When the estate agent had shown them round, they had turned up their noses at the new décor, but they loved the study and said they would restore the rest of the house the same way. Gus loved them already. And it meant he wouldn't have to resort to haunting the house, not that he could anyway, though on the other hand, it would have been nice to scare people – just a little. Ghosts did that sort of thing, didn't they? Perhaps he would scare the little girl. But it wasn't very nice to frighten children. Maybe a small scare wouldn't hurt.

Gus glided down the stairs to greet them. Dad walked in first, with a big, beaming face, followed by Mum and lastly, the little girl, whose face was pinched and purple.

"Alice, don't cry, darling. I thought you liked the house," Mum said, putting an arm around her.

"I do...it's just so far away. I miss my friends."

"You'll make some new ones soon," Mum said.

A toot toot interrupted them.

"That's the removal van. Your dad and I had better go and start sorting things out," Mum said, kissing Alice on the top of her head.

Gus didn't think it was a very good time for a scare – even a small one. He wished he had stayed in the study now.

"Who are you?" Alice said.

"Me?" Gus pointed to his chest.

"Yes, you."

"You can hear me?"

"Yes. Do you live here too?" she asked and

walked closer, clearly curious now.

"Sort of. I'm a ghost," Gus puffed out his chest with pride.

A smile tugged at the corner of Alice's mouth. The smile spread quickly, followed by a giggle and then she couldn't stop laughing. She hugged her stomach and tears ran down her cheeks.

Gus looked hurt.

"I'm sorry. It's just you look so funny with that stringy vest thing, not what I thought a ghost would look like at all."

Gus pulled at his vest. He frowned. Now he didn't even look like a ghost. And just wait 'til she found out how he'd died. He really couldn't do anything right.

"Did you die hundreds of years ago? Were you killed in a sword fight? Or did a lion bite your head off?"

Gus shook his head and found himself telling her how useless he was, how he couldn't even die properly. He told Alice about getting up that Monday morning, just the same as any other. He had stuck his arms in his string vest, gone to pull it over his head and that was as far as he had got. The vest had stuck rigid and refused to move. Then the doorbell had rung. Gus had dashed out of the room and to the top of the stairs, yanking at his vest.

Alice guessed what happened next.

"Yes, you're right. I fell down the stairs."

"I bet that radiator smashed your head in, didn't it?"

"Yes, you could say that," Gus said and touched the gash on his forehead.

"Cool."

They both sat down on the stairs, oblivious to the removal men lugging furniture up and down, Dad shouting orders and Mum fussing round.

Alice told him how sad she was, about her dad's job taking them miles away from all her friends and her school. Her dad was always busy working and Mum was having another baby soon and wouldn't have time for Alice anymore. And the worst thing of all, was that the baby was going to be a horrid little boy who ate worms and wanted to play stupid shooting games.

"Your mum loves you, Alice. I can see that. She'll always have time for you, though if the baby does turn out to be horrible I shall just have to scare him silly. But I'm going to need your help, Alice. I'm not very good at being scary. I'm not very good at anything."

"Yes, you are. You're very good at being a friend," Alice said, smiling.

Gus smiled too. A very wide smile.

About The Author

Esther has always loved words and writing, but she started out working with figures in a bank. She was on an accelerated training programme and studying banking exams, which meant she didn't have time for writing so it wasn't long before it was a thing of the past – or so Esther thought. Her love affair with writing ignited again when she had a serious injury to her back. It meant she could no longer carry out her job working in the bank and it led her back to writing, which has become a daily part of her life.

She has now been working as a freelance writer for nearly twenty years, regularly writing articles and short stories for magazines and newspapers such as *Freelance Market News, Writers' Forum, Writing Magazine, The Guardian, Best of British, The Cat,* and *The People's Friend* to name a few.

Winner of *Writing Magazine, Writers' News* and several other writing competitions and awards, Esther has also had the privilege of judging writing competitions.

As well as working as a freelance writer, she has branched out into the exciting world of copywriting, providing copy for sales letters, brochures, leaflets, web pages, slogans and e-mails.

Esther loves writing but equally she enjoys helping others, which she achieves in her role as a tutor for *The Writers Bureau.* She feels like a proud parent when one of her students has a piece of writing published. Some of them have gone on to become published authors and have achieved great success.

In addition to tutoring Esther works as a freelance copyeditor offering an editing, guidance and advice service for authors and writers. She has edited novels, non-fiction books, articles and short stories. You can find out more about it here: https://esthernewtonblog.wordpress.com/guidance-and-advice/

If you'd like Esther's help, or would like to know more about what she can do for you, please get in touch: estherchilton@gmail.com

Other links:

Blog: https://esthernewtonblog.wordpress.com

Twitter: Esther Chilton - @esthernewton201

Facebook: Esther Chilton

LinkedIn: Esther Chilton

Printed in Poland
by Amazon Fulfillment
Poland Sp. z o.o., Wrocław